WOLF'S CLAIM

THE ROYAL HEIR TRILOGY

JEN L. GREY

Copyright © 2020 by Jen L. Grey

All rights reserved.

No part of this book may be reproduced in any form or by any electronic or mechanical means, including information storage and retrieval systems, without written permission from the author, except for the use of brief quotations in a book review.

CHAPTER ONE

I ENTERED the living room of our new brownstone home and found Kassie, Mona, and Tommy there. "I need to go out and meet Matteo at the restaurant." It was time to give the alpha a heads-up that someone was threatening me here in NYC. The last time it had happened, the vampire prince attacked one of his pack members, and we had to bring the witch, Rose, to heal her.

A Manhattan map lay in the center of a dark cherry coffee table, and Kassie sat on the beige leather couch, leaning over, examining it like it would reveal some sort of treasure.

Tommy sat close to her. I was glad they were finally able to put their differences aside. Both he and Kassie rarely got along, having had some sort of rivalry since they had both been tasked with guarding my father, King Corey, prior to his death.

"There's no way in hell." Kassie's dark amber eyes raised to meet mine. "There is some looney out there, looking for you." Her short black hair managed to bob with her jerky movements.

"Kassie." Mona stood across from them, right underneath the flat screen. She arched her eyebrows so they were hidden under her blonde bangs as she narrowed her brown eyes. "You know better."

"I'm not sure if it bothers me worse when you or Tommy does that." Kassie pouted as she glared at Tommy.

"Hey, I didn't do anything this time." Tommy tugged at his salt and pepper mustache that matched the hair on his head. His dark brown eyes stayed focused on the map as he stretched out his back. "Don't get me involved."

Mona and Kassie were the reason I didn't die with my parents almost thirteen years ago. My uncle, Darren, had wanted to be king so badly that he killed his own brother and attempted to kill his brother's family. Little had he know I had been hidden away and survived.

"You look gorgeous in that dress." Mason walked out of our bedroom in a black suit that molded to his muscles in all the right ways. He was my fated mate and provided the perfect balance I needed. His short, dark hair was a little longer than normal, and his emerald green eyes scanned over me. "The way the red contrasts with your hair is sexy as hell." He walked over to me and pulled me into his hard chest. "Do we have to go? I could think of better ways to spend our time." His lips captured mine, releasing some of the tension in my shoulders.

I wish we could. His lips undid me. Hell, looking at him made me feel things, and I hoped that would never change. Images of last night flashed through my mind. He'd done things to me that I never thought possible. Every time was better than the last, and our bond grew stronger with every passing day.

"If that is a consideration, I say no. Despite the horror it brings to mind telling you this, you should go get it on."

Kassie lifted her chin and frowned. "It's not safe outside of this house."

Now, that I didn't expect. Mason chuckled as he brushed his lips against mine once more.

The doorbell rang, causing a wolf howl to fill the entire house.

Ella descended the stairs from where the other five bedrooms were located and entered the living room. Her blonde hair bounced with each step, and her hazel eyes lit up. "I told you that would make an epic ring. So much better than any other place has."

"It's kind of annoying." Louis appeared right behind her. Together, they went over and sat on the other section of the L-shaped couch.

"Let me go grab the door." Mason shook his head and turned toward to the door. "Is anyone expecting someone?"

"Nope." Ella sat back in the seat and placed her feet on the coffee table.

"What the hell are you doing?" Kassie reached over and smacked her legs. "This is a map."

"What?" Ella pointed at the television. "Elena didn't tell us they were going out, so I had plans to be comfortable and veg out. You can get a new map later."

"If you weren't the King's sister ..." Kassie growled.

Tommy pulled out his walkie talkie and shook his head. "My King, one second." He hurried over and pressed the button down. "Anyone know who's out front?"

There was a pause before a voice got back on the line. "It's ..." He cleared his throat. "It's King Adelmo."

Well, there go those dinner plans. Louis must have told him where we lived. I turned around and pointed at him. "Why didn't you warn us?" I'd hoped that Louis had taken care of this. He was the Prince of Europe and had submitted to me prior to he and Ella sealing their mate bond. His dad had been calling him when we were trying to save Alec. I figured Louis would eventually talk to him and figure this shit out.

"I didn't know." His gray eyes landed on the ground.

"Have you talked to him?" Ella arched an eyebrow and reached over, taking some popcorn out of the bowl he was holding.

"Not exactly." Louis ran his hands through his medium blond hair and sighed. "I was still thinking about what to say."

Great, this is going to go over well. I glanced at Mason. *Do you mind calling Matteo and letting him know we won't be there?*

Fine, but I'll be right back. He hurried off into the bedroom and shut the door.

"Ha, here I was thinking I'd miss out on dinner." Ella removed her feet from the table and turned her body in my direction. "But at least, I'm still getting a good show."

"You can be a real pain in the ass." Her antics always cracked me up, but right now we had more important things to face. "You." I pointed to Louis. "You're going to have to confront him. This isn't on me."

He huffed and placed the popcorn bowl on the table. "Fine."

"For the love of God," Kassie grumbled and lifted the bowl off the table to remove the map. "We'll have to do this another time. Between Ella's nasty feet and the butter from the popcorn, I better move it."

"My feet aren't dirty." Ella stuck out her tongue at Kassie.

"Should we let him in?" Tommy glanced in my direction.

"Yes." I didn't have time for this, but if Louis had been avoiding him for the past several weeks, that wasn't good. Him doing that was only going to make their disagreement worse. "Let's get this over with."

"Okay." Tommy walked over to the door and opened it.

King Adelmo burst through the door, and surprisingly, his gaze didn't land on me. Instead, he scanned the room, obviously looking for his son. "Louis. Get your shit together. You're coming home."

"No, I'm not." Louis took a deep breath and leveled his eyes on his father. "How did you find out where we were?"

They looked so similar. The king's hair was a shade lighter than Louis's blond, but the rest of their features resembled each other.

"That wasn't a question, and I tracked your phone." His father's nostrils flared, and his hands clenched into fists. His tone was laced with alpha power. "I said we're leaving now."

"You know that won't work on me anymore." Louis straightened his shoulders and met his dad's gaze head-on. "You're not my alpha."

Yeah, that's not helping anything. I wasn't sure what the hell I should do. "King Adelmo ..."

"Stop." His eyes landed on mine and were full of rage. "You've done more than enough."

My first reaction was to tell him where to go, but I could only imagine what he was going through right now. "I didn't do anything that warrants your hatred."

"Like hell." His father's European accent became extremely thick. "I thought he'd finally see things if he stayed here for a while. He was supposed to learn how our packs were stronger and respect everything our family has sacrificed. Instead, he submitted to you." A growl laced his final words.

"Though my reign is new, my packs will be stronger in no time." I got that he was upset, but he had no right to come in here and insult me. "I'll do whatever it takes to make sure I protect my own."

"From what I've heard, you've had vampires attack and almost died a month ago." His gray eyes seemed to slice through me. "Some strong leader you are."

"But what you may not have heard is that because of her dedication and willingness to fight, she's already had the major alphas in the larger cities submit to her." Mason appeared back in the room and stood beside me, facing the king. "It's insulting that you'd talk so poorly of us when we're doing everything we can and even hosted your son here for over two months. One more word about my mate, and I'll personally make sure you're kicked out."

"Did you force him to do this?" The color in the king's face resembled the same shade of red as a tomato. "And I actually had thought you might be better than your deadbeat uncle. At least, with him, he'd betrayed me to my face and not behind my back."

"I did not betray you." I could only be sympathetic to a point. He was now overstepping a boundary. "If you keep accusing me in my own home, I'll have my guards kick your ass out."

"And now, both of you have the audacity to threaten me?" He lifted his hand as if he was considering slapping me.

Mason stepped in front of me, his back brushing against my chest. "I'd put that hand down before you do something you'll regret." Mason's words were almost indistinguishable, given how thick his growl had become.

"Dad, stop." Louis finally walked over and stood next to me. "She had nothing to do with this."

"Bollocks!" The king yelled so loud it echoed against the walls. "A prince doesn't submit to another royal without something being held over their head." He pointed his finger in Louis's direction. "Your mother is beside herself with grief. It's time for you to come home."

"I am home." Louis took a deep breath and stared his father down. "You know Henry is better suited for the throne anyway."

"It doesn't matter who I think is best fit." King Adelmo took a step into Louis's personal space. "Destiny chooses the next heir. What are you going to do? Live with them," he said as he pointed at Mason and me, "the rest of your life?" He waved his hands. "Get your shit. We're going."

This wasn't going to end well.

"Why don't you back off?" Ella got to her feet and rushed over to stand between me and her mate. "He doesn't want to go."

"This is what's wrong with you." The king's eyes landed on me. "You blackmail my son, the next in line to be king, and you let some pack member speak to me so rudely. Your father would be ashamed."

Those words were like a slap to my face. It hurt me deep within my soul.

"You arrogant asshole ..." Ella started, but Mason raised a hand.

"You come here unannounced, and yet my mate allowed you in." Mason's voice grew soft ... scary. "She allowed you to act in anger, understanding that you are hurt, and then you purposefully say the one thing that would cause her pain." He stepped right into the King's face and stared him straight in the eyes. "Get the fuck out of this house now. You're not welcome back. If you want to talk with your son, call him. Until you apologize, you aren't welcome here any longer."

"Now you listen here ..." The king started to back up but was cut short when Tommy, Kassie, and Mona passed by me to surround him. "You can't be serious. Do you know the repercussions of kicking me out?"

I couldn't allow him to think I was weak even if he'd ripped my heart out. "Do you know the repercussions of coming into my house to falsely accuse me and my mate of extortion?" I took a deep breath and straightened my shoulders. "Like the King said," insisted as I pointed to Mason, "get the fuck out now. If you don't, our guards will make you."

Realization seemed to settle on him as he stumbled back a step and blinked a few times. "Louis, get your things now."

Louis reached out and took Ella's hand. "I've pledged my loyalty to them ..." He paused and glanced right at me. "To her. This is my home now."

"What's wrong?" Kassie's voice had a hard edge. "Didn't you want him to marry an American anyway?"

When he first found out I was alive, that was the expectation that he had set. That Louis and I would marry.

"I can't believe this." He turned on his heel and headed to the front door. He glanced over his shoulder. "I'll find out what you're using in order to keep him here. You're obviously using her," he said as his eyes landed on Ella, "but there has to be something else too. He wouldn't do this for a quick lay."

"You don't get to talk about her that way." Louis's shoulders stiffened, and his nostrils flared as he stepped in front of Ella.

"Get out now." Mason took a step in the king's direction.

"This is your last chance or I'll personally kick your ass out in the next second."

The king harrumphed and opened the door, slamming it shut in his wake.

Are you okay? Mason turned to me and pulled me into his arms.

I couldn't cry. Not right now. Yes, all of these people were my family now. Yet, I was afraid if I started crying, I wasn't quite sure when I'd stop. *I'll be fine.*

"My dad's an ass." Louis frowned as his eyes scanned over me. "He's a difficult person to understand. Hell, I never understood him."

I tugged myself out of Mason's arms and narrowed my eyes directly at the prince. "He sure meant every word he said."

"Gotta side with her on this one, babe." Ella shrugged and let go of his hand, standing closer to me.

"You do know you don't have to step closer to her to take her side, right?" Mason arched an eyebrow at his sister.

"It's better for theatrics." She winked at me. "It drives the point home better."

"I just need to make sure." I took a deep breath and stared him down. "You don't feel like you have to stay here, right? Because of Ella." Even if we hadn't meant to blackmail him, what if he was afraid of our reaction if they left. He didn't want to take her away from her family.

"Honestly, it might be nice to have a little bit of a break from her, at least from time to time." Mason leaned over and placed his chin on the top of my head. "So maybe you could reconsider."

"No, that's not it." Louis sighed and took a deep breath. "It's that the two of you make amazing leaders. You're not even half my father's age, and you both understand what a true leader is. It's not asking someone to do something you aren't willing to do yourself." He huffed and shook his head. "Dad never goes out on reconnaissance or takes part in any fights that we have against witches or vampires. He stays safe, sitting in his castle."

I wasn't expecting that. I wasn't quite sure what else to say.

"I understand if I need to move out and find my own place." He took a deep breath and sighed. "I'd been thinking about that the past couple weeks, but with the recent threat, I'd planned to hold off."

"You need to stay here for now." There was no way I'd want Ella and him to put themselves out there as easy targets. "We can figure the rest of this out later. Right now, we need to warn the packs and visit the ones we haven't been able to yet."

A phone rang, and Kassie pulled hers from her pocket. "Hello?"

There was no telling what King Adelmo had done. My stomach churned as I waited for her to end the call.

"I'll be there shortly." Kassie hung up the call, and her forehead lined with worry.

"What's going on?" She just needed to tell me.

"We've got a problem." Kassie paused, but her eyes locked with Tommy's. "Richard and Debra have escaped from prison."

At first, the words didn't make sense. "My cousin and aunt?" That couldn't be possible. They hated my guts, and we had them locked up in the most secure location.

"Yes."

Someone had to have helped them to escape, and I had no clue who it could have been.

CHAPTER TWO

OUT OF ALL THE possibilities that had run through my head, my aunt and cousin escaping wasn't one of them. "Both of them?" I probably sounded like a parrot right now.

"Get the guards to track their scents." Mason took off his suit jacket and threw it on a chair. "This is ridiculous. If they can't do it, I will."

"Whoa, there." Tommy lifted his hand. "I can't have the royal I'm protecting running straight into enemy lines."

"It's our prison." I was with Mason on this one. "We're going."

"Of course they are." Kassie sighed and shook her head.

"If it was anyone else but her, you'd be impressed." Mona snorted as she patted Kassie on the shoulder. "And really, we only have ourselves to blame."

That was true. They'd trained my ass on self-defense and proper weapon usage over the past twelve years. "I promise to not run off unprompted."

"Girl, you don't think we noticed the last word of that sentence?" Ella rolled her eyes and leaned against Louis's shoulder. "That wasn't even worth promising."

"It only makes it worse." Louis nodded his head in agreement.

"I think I liked you better before this ..." I said as I waved my hands between the two of them, "happened."

"You and me both." Mason sighed. *I got the pleasure of walking in on them one night.*

What? How do I not know about that? It was better him than me.

It was in the apartment before we moved here. He stepped closer to me. *When you were injured.* His green eyes scanned my face.

That was before we moved into this place. The vampire prince had his eyes set on killing Mason, and I'd jumped in front of him, taking the dagger in my heart. I should've died, but hell, I got to visit my parents in what could only be the realm between life and death. Somehow, I had gotten enough of the vampire prince's blood in my system to save me from death. I had been able to protect Mason and see my parents once more, which made everything that happened worth it. However, I'd never have admitted it to Mason.

"Let's go," Kassie growled the words.

"I'll pull the car out of the garage and get it started." Tommy ran out the front door, scanning the area as if Richard and Debra were going to appear right there.

"Damn him," Kassie grumbled as she ran after him with her hand on the side of her hip to easily grab her gun if needed.

"Go on." Mona pointed to the door. "I'll take the back."

"Hell, yeah." Ella hurried out the door first. "This is so much better than a movie."

"Something isn't right with her." Mason shook his head and glared at Louis. "You need to keep her in line."

"Oh, like you do Elena?" Louis smirked and shrugged his shoulders. "Criticize me after you're able to do that with her." His gaze landed right on me.

"Don't even try." As fun as this was, I needed to get to the prison and fast. I hurried to the door, leaving all three of them behind.

"See." Louis chuckled. "She just left your ass too."

"Not funny." Mason rushed and caught up to me as I climbed into the Suburban.

Mona stood right by the door, scanning the area for any threats.

I went straight in so that I was sitting in the middle row, then Louis and Mona could climb in the back.

"Let me get in first." Louis jumped in front of Mason and clambered into the vehicle, crouching low as he made his way to the back seat next to Ella.

It wasn't long before Mona and Mason got in, and Tommy took off to wherever we kept prisoners.

Mona groaned, and a hard slap could be heard from the back. "Don't make me do another hand check while I'm back here."

I didn't even want to touch this one. "How far away is this place?" The longer it took us to get there, the harder it was going to be to find them.

"Not far." Kassie glanced over her shoulder from the front passenger seat.

"But this is the heart of NYC." The fact that I didn't know the location of the prison was super disturbing.

"Actually, you were living right above it and didn't know." Tommy glanced in the rearview mirror.

The NYC apartment's modern building we'd moved from appeared in front of us.

"Are you talking about that?" I pointed to the building.

They had to be, but that didn't make sense. That was starkly different than a prison.

"What you might not know is that you own the entire building." Tommy turned into the parking garage beneath the building.

It was one of the most luxurious accommodations, especially compared to our new home. Here, there was a parking garage, whereas our new home was lucky to have the single car garage that the guards insisted on.

"You don't rent out the basement." Mona leaned forward, trying to gain some distance from the two in the back. "And we use it as a holding ground of sorts."

"So there really isn't a prison?" Mason's forehead lined, and his brows furrowed. "That doesn't make a lot of sense."

"Actually, it does." Kassie turned around and met Mason's eyes. "Your guards are the best trained in the entire world. We should be the ones over the security."

"Fat lot of good it did for tonight." Ella snorted and shook her head. "I wouldn't be bragging like that when two escaped."

She had a point, but now wasn't the time to voice it. I glanced over my shoulder to see that Louis was frowning at her and had to be speaking to her mentally. Sometimes, I forgot he was a good ally to have. He understood the politics of it all.

"Anyway." Mason's words were brash. "How many people are down there?"

"Not many." Tommy rolled the window down and reached out, scanning his badge. "Normally, packs take care of their own when it comes to disobedience. So we have the stragglers like Richard and Debra down there."

"Besides them, there's only one more prisoner down there, and she's a little off." Mona shook her head.

"That's one way of putting it." Kassie laughed hard. "Or you can just say damn crazy."

"She tried killing your mom after your parents mated." Mona shook her head. "She'd been obsessed with your father and thought she deserved to be Queen."

"Wow, things that I never expected to hear." They'd never mentioned anything like that to me before.

"It hurt your father dearly." Tommy frowned and put the car in PARK. "They grew up together. She was even his high school sweetheart."

"And he had no clue whatsoever that she was insane?" This almost sounded like a movie or something you'd find on Netflix.

"Not a single one." Kassie opened the door and got out.

Within a few minutes, we were heading toward the familiar elevator we'd normally take up to the apartment. We followed Tommy inside, and he badged again, hitting the letter B.

Do not do anything stupid here. Mason wrapped his arms around me, pulling me back so I was leaning against his chest. *I almost lost you once. I'm not sure if I could survive a second time.*

Even though we hadn't discussed it, through our bond, I felt his guilt. He blamed himself for my near miss with death. I had even tried explaining to him that it wasn't his fault, but he wouldn't let it go. *I'll stay right by your side.* I had every intention of doing that.

As I stepped out onto the cool, basement floor, it hit me. I hadn't changed out of my stupid dress. This was going to be fun. I could run upstairs and change, but it would only waste more time. I'd just have to suck it up and deal.

The walls in the hallway were white, and the lighting was dim. It was obvious that we were underground. In the front was a younger guard whose mouth opened and closed as he stared at us from behind a large desk with computer monitors all around it. He had to be close to our age.

"Josh." Tommy nodded his head at the young man. "Where is everyone else?"

"They're ..." He cleared his throat and tugged on the neckline of his black shirt. His longish brown hair was plastered to his forehead, and his golden eyes seemed to glow. "In Richard's and Debra's rooms, trying to figure out what happened."

"Why aren't you tracing the scent?" Mason stepped forward and glared at the guard. His body was tense, and I placed my hand inside his, squeezing comfortingly.

"It doesn't matter." The last thing we needed to do was berate Josh and make him feel worse than he already did. "Let's get to it."

"You're going to do it?" Josh blinked his eyes at me.

"What the hell does that mean?" Ella pushed through Mason and me to the front. "I bet she could kick your ass." She nudged me on my shoulder. "Go ahead. Do it. Make the little bitch cry."

"No. No." He shook his head from side to side. "I didn't mean it like that." He raised a finger and pointed at me. "It's her dress."

"Don't take offense to her." Louis grabbed Ella's waist and pulled her back. "Her mouth runs away with her at times."

"Did you really just say that?" Ella's eyes widened, and the green in her hazel eyes was hidden by their darkening color.

"We don't have time for this." Kassie waved her off. "Let's go."

"Yeah, okay." The guy reached over to push a button, and there was a loud buzz. "You're ready to go."

Our group followed Kassie down the hallway and through a large set of steel double-doors.

It was similar in the cement vibe, but there was just a long hallway of steel doors that were all secured, giving it kind of a hospital feel as well. We walked about halfway down when we came to a spot where two doors were opened, side by side.

There was a guard in each of them.

"Any clues yet?" Mona walked into the room where an older woman was searching for a clue or anything that stood out from the norm.

"Not a one." She blew out her breath and placed her hands on her hips. "I don't get it. It's like they just vanished."

"Same over here." The guard from the other room shouted. Frustration was evident in his voice. "I don't know what to do."

I entered the same room as Mona and took a deep breath, filling my lungs. I could smell Richard in here but nothing else. "So he had to get out by himself."

"That's not possible." Tommy marched into the room. "It would be hard enough for him to get out but with his mother too?"

"What about the cameras?" Kassie and the other guard walked into the room with us. "Didn't they see anything?"

"No." The male guard's shoulders sagged. "It was like they all blacked out. We thought it was a technical issue."

"Did the other prisoner see anything?" Mason's body was tense and ready to pounce.

"Well, yeah. Kind of." The lady ran her hand through her dark brown hair. "Gabby was loose in the hallway when we got here."

"Is that the girl who had the hots for your dad?" Ella glanced down the hallway like she might appear.

"She means the former king." Louis shook his head and grinned.

"They knew what she meant." Kassie rolled her eyes and focused on the guard. "What did she say?"

"She hasn't been really forthcoming with information." The male guard cringed. "The only place they could've exited was the stairwell."

"You're right, but how?" Tommy headed out of the room and turned down the hallway in the direction where the other exit must have been.

"I'm going with him." Kassie marched out the door and turned to Mona. "Why don't the rest of you go and talk to Gabby. Maybe she'd be willing to talk to someone in this group."

"Okay, let's do this." Mona pulled some keys out of her pocket and walked to the door directly across the hall. She inserted a key, and soon I heard a click.

I need you to stay next to me. Mason snagged my waist and turned me so I was facing him. *I get that this is important and you need to be involved. But don't leave my side. I can't be worried about something happening to you.*

It hurt that he worried so much. *I go where you go.* I stood on my tiptoes and kissed his lips quickly.

He nodded and gripped my hand like he thought I might disappear as we entered the room.

"Well, well ..." A woman who had to be in her mid-forties stood only a few feet shy of the entrance. "This has been such a weird day. I've had so many visitors." She straightened her shoulders, and some of her midnight black hair fell into her face. Her dark mocha eyes skimmed the group, stopping right on me.

"Cut the crap." Mona entered the room and motioned for us to follow her. "Tell us what you know."

"So you're the bitch that she birthed." Gabby sneered and took a few steps toward me. "You have her red hair and his blue eyes. What an abomination."

"She is your queen." Mason moved in front of me, his body ready to fight. "You can't talk to her that way."

"Wow, this girl is whack." Ella murmured behind me, whispering it into Louis's ear.

"Actually, I can, snowflake." Gabby tsked as her eyes scanned him up and down before landing back on me. "Of course, the most attractive man here would be mated to Serafina's spawn."

"Hey, my mate is sexy too." Ella pointed at Louis.

The woman didn't even bother noting her presence. "They said it would be worth it for me to stay back."

"They? Who do you mean?" She seemed fixated on me, so maybe I'd have better luck. I needed Mason to get out of my damn way so I could get some answers.

"Do you think I'm dumb enough to tell you that?" She giggled loudly and looked almost crazed. "Of course you do. I bet you're just like her."

"Like who?" I had a feeling it had to do with Mom.

"The same red hair, the inflated ego, how you expect me to tell you all my deep dark secrets." She pulled at the ends of her hair. "All so superficial, but yet he fell for it."

"They were fated mates. They didn't have a choice." Maybe if I pushed her, she'd start rambling, not thinking through what to say.

Be careful. Mason linked with me and edged even more in front, his back brushing my chest. *She's making me nervous.*

"You see, Corey was mine." She shook her head and spat

at the ground. "I don't understand what he saw in you and not me."

"Holy shit." Louis stood behind me, but even he took a step closer as if she might attack me at any second. "She's merging you with your mother."

These two meatheads were getting on my damn nerves. "This has nothing to do with you and me." If I played the part, would that help? "These people could hurt innocents."

"They don't give a shit about hurting anyone but you." She stumbled toward me and sneered. "Of course it's you. Everything revolves around you. They said I could end it."

You need to leave. Mason's shoulders were tense, and his breathing grew faster.

When I didn't move, his jaw ticked. *Now.*

Like hell I would. I wouldn't leave him alone; we fought together now. *No.*

"See, you aren't even grateful for your mate, who is trying to protect you. That's why I have to do it." An ear-piercing scream filled my ears as Gabby pulled a knife from her pants. Her eyes found mine behind Mason.

"Watch out." Mona cried.

"No." Mason roared as he ran toward Gabby. When he got close to her, she bent and grabbed his arm, throwing him over her body.

"Mason." My eyes stayed locked on him. Just when I was about to run toward him, all hell broke loose.

Mona rushed to get to me, but Ella was in her way, and Gabby was fast. Mason landed on his back, immediately jumping to his feet. The closest people to me were Louis and Ella.

Gabby's eyes locked onto mine, and her aim was clear, the knife targeting my heart. I had no time to move out of the way.

Moments before the blade could hit my chest, Louis jumped in front of me. He took the knife in his upper arm and tackled her to the ground.

"Louis!" Ella cried as she rushed past me.

Mason leaned over and put Gabby into a headlock, causing her eyes to roll back in her head.

Whoever it was that gave her that damn knife, not only did they free Richard and Debra, but they had conspired in an attempt on my life. Yet, how do you fight a faceless enemy that you know nothing about?

CHAPTER THREE

"THAT WASN'T MEANT FOR HIM." Gabby took a ragged breath as she came to and growled. "Why did he do that? Why do people always protect her?"

"You stupid bitch!" Ella screamed the words and reared back, punching her square in the nose. "If he dies, you'll be next."

With the way she was acting, I wouldn't be surprised if she killed Gabby now. "Ella, he needs you." I bent over and frowned. "How bad does it hurt?" The prince had risked his life for mine, which meant more than he'd ever realize.

"Ah ... you know," Louis grunted as he glanced at the dagger that was still protruding from his arm. "Just fucking horrible."

"Cuff her." I flicked my eyes up at my three loyal guards. "Take her into another cell. We'll deal with her after we help him."

Mason leaned over the woman's face and bared his teeth. "We aren't done with you. You tried to kill my mate. You'll be rotting in hell soon if I have anything to do with it."

"Aren't you something?" She rubbed her finger along his

chest and grinned. "We could have fun together."

In a flash, Mason took hold of her fingers and bent them backward, causing her to whimper.

Oh, dear God. I couldn't take much more. "Get her the hell out of here, now."

The woman guard handed Tommy the cuffs, and he took a step in Gabby's direction.

"No, please don't." She tried to stand but stumbled backward, attempting to get away. "She deserved it. Really, she did."

At first, I'd tried to humor her, but now she was getting on my nerves. "I haven't done a damn thing to you. This was our first time ever meeting. If you really did love my dad, why would you want to hurt me, his daughter?"

"That just makes it worse." She wrinkled her nose and jerked, trying to break free from Tommy's hold. "I hope they kill you."

"Take her out," Mason yelled the words, his breathing rapid.

We need her for answers. I understood he was upset, but we couldn't do anything rash.

That's the only reason she's still breathing. Mason stared Gabby down as Tommy pushed her out of the room.

"We need to get the dagger out of Louis." The longer we left it in his arm, the more he would bleed. "I don't know what the hell to do."

"It's not a critical wound." Mona bent down to examine the injury. "Kassie, can you call Gracie? She should be able to handle this."

"On it." Kassie pulled out her phone and stepped into the hallway to make the call.

"The phone works down here?" I was surprised, considering we were surrounded by concrete.

"Connected to Wi-Fi calling." Mona reached for the black handle of the knife. "I'm going to pull this out to stop the bleeding."

"Whoa." Ella grabbed Mona's arm. "Are you sure you know what you're doing?"

"Promise." Mona smiled at her. "Mason, I may need your help since Tommy and Kassie are busy."

"What's up?" He leaned over, wincing as he took in the wound.

"First off, pretty boy," Mona snorted, "you might get some blood on those nice slacks if you aren't careful."

"Okay." He nodded and lifted an arm over his head, stretching it out. "Damn, she threw me over her body. I'm going to be sore tomorrow."

"Stop whining and get down here to help." Mona shook her head as she adjusted her grip on the knife once again.

"Do you need my help?" I hated being worthless, and Louis had saved my life. If it hadn't been for him, she would've hit her mark.

You've done enough. Mason's tone was low and angry.

What the hell does that mean? He was acting like this was my damn fault.

"Not from you." Mona tilted her head in my direction. "That dress doesn't look like it's very comfortable."

That was an understatement. This was just another excuse I could use to not wear one since people attacking us seemed to be a common occurrence nowadays.

"I can help." Ella bent down, flaunting her jeans and shirt at me.

Not really, but it still felt that way at the moment.

"Maybe you shouldn't." Louis backed away, causing the dagger to dig more deeply into his arm since Mona was gripping it. "Ow ... Dammit."

"Well, don't move." Mona shook her head as Mason squatted beside her. "Mason, hold on tightly to his arm."

"Why don't you hold his hand?" Mason glanced at his sister. He pointed at Louis's uninjured arm and then gripped the prince's shoulder tight. "I bet this is going to hurt like a bitch."

"Wow, thanks for the comforting words." Louis frowned and wrinkled his nose. "It's hurting pretty bad right now."

"Then, I guess you better buckle up." Ella took his hand and grabbed his chin, turning his head so he was looking at her.

"You better be glad I love you." Louis narrowed his eyes. "Because if it was anyone else, I'd kick their ass for doing that."

Kassie walked back into the room. "She's on her way." She cringed when she saw what was about to go down. "Oh, damn. That's going to hurt."

"Really?" Louis pouted and growled. "Do you people honestly need to keep telling me this?"

Both Ella and Mason's eyes were on Mona, and she gave them a slight nod. Then, the three of them worked like clockwork. Mona jerked the dagger out of Louis's arm as Mason clamped down, preventing his arm from moving."

"Agh!" An ear pounding screech left Louis, and he sagged against Ella. Tears ran down his face.

"I'm so sorry, baby." Ella reached over and placed his head in her lap. "But that had to happen."

"Some warning would've been nice." His voice was low and raspy.

"I promise they did you a favor." Kassie walked out into the hallway, and after a few moments, she stepped back in. "Here." She tossed a clean white towel at Mona.

"Thanks." Mona pushed it against the wound, and even

then, blood stained the material. "We need to get him upstairs to the apartment. That's where Gracie will go."

"Can you walk?" Mason released his arm and glanced at the bottom of his pants. "Man, I thought I was careful."

A huge spot of blood had soaked the bottom of his pants leg where he'd stepped through it.

"My shoulder is hurting, not my legs." He lifted his head from Ella's lap and clutched the injured arm. "Damn, I need some whiskey or something."

Ella scrambled to her feet. "Here, let me help you." She bent down and grabbed his uninjured arm.

"No, I've got it." He took a deep breath, and his face began turning a shade pale. "I thought it would hurt less."

"You didn't tell him." Kassie chuckled. "Smart woman."

"Thanks." Mona arched an eyebrow and pursed her lips. "Sometimes, it's good if you let me have my secrets."

"Well, I'm glad she didn't," Louis said as he stood on his feet and clutched his free hand to his side. "I wouldn't have let her do it otherwise."

"And that's actually why she did it." Those two women were amazing and knew how to get people to listen to them.

"Let's get you upstairs. She should be here soon." Mona patted Louis's back, and they filed out. As I moved to follow, I noticed that the mate bond link between Mason and me was blocked. A chill ran through me.

As I turned toward him, I confirmed what I already knew. His jaw was clenched, his eyes were tight, and he was scowling at me.

"Mason ..." I'd never seen him look that way at me before.

"No, don't." He shook his head. "Not now. The most important priority is getting Louis medical care since he was injured to protect you."

"I didn't mean ..."

"Save it, Elena." He brushed past me and paused to look at me one last time. "I can't talk to you right now." He turned his back to me and followed the group, leaving me behind.

Angry tears threatened to pool in my eyes, and my heart ached at the loss of our connection.

A warm hand touched my shoulder, causing me to startle.

"Sorry, I didn't mean to scare you." Tommy's deep voice brought comfort. "Gabby is locked in and settled into her new room."

"Did she say anything else?" We had to figure out who this new enemy was. Obviously, they knew where to hit me.

"No, she didn't other than her usual crazy mumblings." He gave me a sad grin.

"Okay, thank you." I needed to catch up with the others and make sure Louis was okay. Hell, that prince was growing on me more and more each day. After this, I didn't think I could think of him as anything but family.

"He's hurting."

"I know. Gracie should be here soon to take care of him." I took a step when his hand caught me once more.

"No, I meant Mason." Tommy dropped his hand and licked his bottom lip. "Your father and mother had the same argument at least once a year."

"Really?" I had always remembered them as being happy and loving with one another.

"It's because they loved each other so much." He sighed and stared down the hall as if his mind had gone to another place. "Being a royal, you have to know when to stand tall and when to back down."

"I couldn't back down with her ..."

"Oh, I agree ... but I'm talking about Mason." He tilted

his head to the side and gave me a huge smile. "Your parents would be so proud of you."

"What?" I hadn't been expecting that.

"You know right from wrong and truly care. Your father wanted his brothers to feel and understand that same sentiment, but they never did. He'd be so proud to see you now." He took a few steps closer to me and laughed. "You care more than he ever did, and you understand things in ways that he never could."

"And he knew how to rule without messing up every few days." No matter which way I went, someone wound up getting hurt—Alec, Louis, Mona, Kassie, and Mason. They'd all been attacked in one way or another because of me. "I should've never let them get so close. They just get hurt because of me."

"They're the reason you're as strong as you are." Tommy nodded his head toward the door, and we began walking at a snail's pace. "He just needs time. He'll come around."

"Will he?" Even though we were fated mates, that didn't mean we had to be together. Fated mates rarely die at the same time, and the other can still live a normal and happy-ish life. If he wanted, he could walk away. "You know what they say. There is a thin line between love and hate."

"That's what humans say." Tommy chuckled and shook his head. "That doesn't really work with mates."

"You never know." Mason had never been so cold to me before.

"Oh, I do." He opened the door for me and waved me through. "Just give him some time to process. He won't be able to stay away from you for long."

Yeah, I doubted that.

When we entered the apartment, there was a short woman standing in the foyer with Mona.

"Here is Queen Elena." Mona waved toward me.

"Your Highness." The girl bowed her head, causing her carrot red hair to fall, framing her face. "It's so nice to meet you even though I wish it was under better circumstances." When she raised her face to meet mine, her light green eyes stared into mine.

"Gracie." That's the only person I could reconcile with her. At this point, I doubted they'd let anyone else into the house right now.

"She just got here." Mona pointed at the big black bag. "I was giving her a brief update on what happened."

"I'm so glad you didn't get harmed." She gave me a small, forced smile.

"Thanks, I just wish none of us had gotten injured." It didn't seem right to say thank you. "Is he in the living room?"

"Yeah, let's go." Mona led the way.

"I'm going to head into the kitchen to grab a drink." Tommy nodded as he peeled off from us.

When we stepped into the den, Ella and Louis were on the couch.

I scanned the room and didn't find Mason. Did he already leave? "Where's Mason?"

"He's out there." Ella pointed to the balcony. "Pouting."

"Let's take a look at your arm." Gracie walked over to Louis and gave him a small smile. "I'm here to stitch you up."

"What ... I won't heal?" Louis pouted as he stared at her bag.

"You will, but it'll leave less of a scar if we stitch it closed. I'll come by in two days to remove the stitches too."

That was one of the nice things about being a shifter. We did heal fast.

"Fine." Louis removed the towel so she could inspect the wound. "I need to look my best for my baby." With a smirk, he winked at Ella.

Right then, I was envious of their flirting. "If you guys don't mind, I'm going out onto the balcony." Now that Louis was getting taken care of, I wanted to go ahead and get things cleared up between Mason and me.

"We'll let you know if we need anything." Kassie waved me off.

It only took a few strides to reach the balcony door. It connected around the side of the apartment, and there were stairs that led up to the balcony attached to our bedroom.

When I stepped outside, I didn't see him but could smell his scent in the air. I took a deep breath of his signature earthy smell and followed it up the stairs. I found him in our normal spot, sitting on the large loveseat, staring at the lights of the city that never sleeps. "Hey."

He took a deep breath and glanced behind him. "Hey."

"Can I join you?" I'd never felt like I had to ask before, and it bothered me.

"Yeah." He patted the open seat next to him. "I was hoping you'd come find me."

"Well, at least, there's that." I slowly walked over and sat next to him. "You said you wanted to talk."

"Yeah, I did." He sighed and placed his head in his hands. "But I don't know anymore. Why didn't you leave when I asked you to?"

"Because I needed answers. If I left every time I didn't want to hear or do something, I'd never get anything accomplished." I needed him to understand.

"But I asked you to." He lifted his head and sighed. "Do you have a death wish?"

"What? No." Did he think I was insane? Wait, I probably didn't want to know the answer to that question.

"It sure seems like it." He reached over and tugged me into his chest. "How many times do I have to watch you almost die?"

"But I didn't."

"Only because of Louis." He reached over and brushed his fingers along my cheek. "I can't keep almost losing you." He leaned over and pressed his lips to mine. Then, he pulled back ever so slightly. "You need an entire bulletproof suit."

A giggle escaped. "I'm sorry. I didn't know that was going to happen. I don't like my near-death experiences either. Maybe I'm like a cat."

"Well, if so, you're out of half your lives." He kissed me and opened our bond back up.

His feelings of love, devotion, and fear filled the empty hole he had created. "It's not fun being cut off." I had to at least admit that to him.

"Yeah, I know that feeling all too well." He kissed me again, his feelings colliding with mine. He growled as his hands dug into the sides of my dress. He grabbed my waist and pulled me on top of him. "I love you so damn much."

"I love you."

His fingers inched under my dress, and soon my body began to respond.

I couldn't hold back my moan. "We need to go to our bedroom." There were weirdos all over the city, and I didn't want anyone, even accidentally, seeing us. *I need you now.*

"Fine." He wrapped his arms around my waist and hoisted my legs around him.

It was only a minute before he had the door to our bedroom opened and was letting me fall back onto the bed, my red hair cascading over the covers. He bent over me, kissed my lips, and then deepened the kiss.

As I attempted to pull him down on top of me, he leaned back. *I've got blood all over my pants. Do you feel like a shower?*

That sounds perfect.

He reached under me, lifting me again, and our mouths connected. As I sucked on his tongue, he carried me to the bathroom.

Stumbling through the bathroom door, he felt his way into the large walk-in shower and then put my feet back on the ground.

I reached around him, turning the water on.

Despite the cold temperature, it did nothing to cool the fire between us.

His hands dug into my sides as he reached around me to unzip my dress. In one quick motion, he pulled the dress down my hips and tossed it to the floor. *You're so damn beautiful.*

Your outfit is ruined. Grasping the front of his shirt, I ripped it open, and the buttons flew everywhere as I pushed it off and tossed it down next to my dress.

My eyes scanned his body and locked on his ink, the wolf pawprint on his upper arm. That tattoo always did something to my insides.

He leaned over me at first, brushing my lips with his, but then began trailing kisses down my neck. My arms wrapped around him, and I dug my nails into his back.

A low growl emanated from his chest. His hands unclasped my bra and cupped my breast, making me moan.

My hands went straight for his pants, removing every article of clothing from his body. He was hard in all the right places.

He pulled me against him once more, trailing kisses down my breast and flicking the nipple in the exact way that I loved.

Our feelings for each other colliding only made me that much more desperate for him. *I can't wait any longer.*

His fingers brushed the inside of my thighs and they slowly trailed up to my waist. He yanked my underwear off, causing it to rip in two.

Once we were naked, I needed to feel him in every way. I wrapped my arms around his neck and climbed up his body, and he thrust inside me.

Each thrust brought me closer and closer to the edge.

The tension from the day vanished, and all that mattered was him and me in this moment. He bent down to nip at my breast as he brought me closer to the edge.

Love you. His words growled in my head as we both climaxed at the exact same time.

We clung to each other as he pushed me so my back was up against the wall. The water was now hot and washing away the evidence of what we'd just done.

It wasn't long before we had bathed each other and crawled into the center of the bed. In this moment, everything felt right in the world, and we couldn't keep our hands off of each other.

We've had a long day and better get some sleep. His voice was like a whisper in my head. He pulled me beside him so that we were spooning. Soon, my eyes grew heavy as I took in his heartbeat and felt our true connection between us. We loved each other so much, and we could never live without one another. I just hoped we could find whoever it was out there hunting me before it was too late.

CHAPTER FOUR

A FEW DAYS passed with nothing happening out of the ordinary, which usually meant something big was brewing if the past few situations had taught me anything. Thankfully, Louis healed. Still, I couldn't help but wonder where and when the next person would get hurt.

We were attempting to head out to Matteo's again. For some reason, going to his restaurant to eat always triggered some kind of attack. The first one had happened to one of his own workers there, a pack member. Then, the next time, my crazy cousin and aunt broke out of prison. Hopefully, this time it would go down without a problem.

"No dress tonight?" Mason appeared from the walk-in closet attached to our bedroom at our brownstone home and stared at my reflection in the mirror.

"Nope." I ran my hands over the black, wide-legged jumpsuit that I'd chosen. "At least, I can move comfortably in this."

"And you still look hot." He made his way over to me and wrapped his arms around my waist. "I'm one lucky man." He kissed down my neck, causing my body to warm.

"You know we can't be late." I turned around to face him, brushing my lips against his. *Maybe we can be a little late.*

"Don't tempt me. But after we had to cancel so suddenly, we'd better not push our luck." He growled and stepped back. "However, if you want to change my mind, just keep looking at me that way."

"So dramatic." I rolled my eyes and decided to press one of his buttons. "I see where Ella learned it from."

He wrinkled his nose and pointed at me. "You knew that was too far. I'll have to punish you later."

"Promises, promises." I walked past him and ran my hand along his black slacks, touching one of my favorite places.

He caught my hand and pulled me into him. "You're not doing a good job of getting out of here." His lips crashed on to mine once more.

"Hey, guys. Are you ..." Ella entered the room and stopped in her tracks. "Eww." She huffed the rest of the way to step between us, pushing us apart. "You're going to mess up your makeup."

I tried calming my breathing. When my eyes landed on Mason, I couldn't help but snort. He had lipstick smeared all around his lips.

"And what have I told you about messing up her makeup?" Ella growled as she headed over to my makeup counter and picked up a cloth. "Wipe the lipstick off your face," she instructed Mason and turned toward me. "And you, fix your lips."

"It's not that bad. I have a neutral color on." I rolled my eyes as I glanced in the mirror. My lipstick was a little smudged. I'd decided to wear dark eyeshadow instead of red lips. I touched it up and turned to her. "Done. Let's go."

"Fine. Louis is waiting for us." She turned on her heels and stopped at the door. "Come on. I'm not leaving the two of you alone or you'll cause us to be late. Louis wouldn't let us be late, so you can't have that kind of fun either."

"All right, Mom," I growled as I took Mason's hand and led him through the bedroom door.

"Is the car pulled out front?" I headed toward the front door when Kassie stepped in front of me, blocking my way.

"No, we can't risk it." Kassie pointed to the door that was at the end of the hallway past the den. "We're going through the garage."

"Still no clue about who broke your aunt and cousin out of jail?" Louis frowned and shook his head. He raised his hand and rubbed his now healed arm.

"Not one." Kassie closed her eyes and wrinkled her nose. "But we'll figure it out.'

"Let's go." Ella had been cooped up in the house all week with the rest of us. She was eager to get out and about. "Dinner is calling."

Within seconds, we were in the car and pulling out.

"If anything looks suspicious," Kassie said from the front passenger seat, "we won't be hanging around. You will all leave immediately. Is that clear?"

"Yes, we know." She'd been lecturing me all morning about not taking unnecessary risks. Apparently, she's on Mason's side about the whole Gabby situation, which doesn't surprise me. At times, she's more protective over me than him.

"Relax." Tommy turned the wheel, heading on to the main road, and then brushed his fingers along Kassie's arm. "It'll be okay. The three of us are going to be there to keep an eye out."

Do the two of them have something going on? Mason

turned his head toward me with an arched eyebrow. *They are acting more and more cordial.*

I was just thinking the same thing. I'd never seen them get along, so that was odd.

"All right, we're pulling up." Mona pulled out her gun in the backseat and checked it.

"Don't point that thing at me," Ella grumbled.

"It's not." Mona shook her head and put it back in its sheath. "Everything looks good back here. What about up there?"

"We're good. Let's go." Kassie climbed out of the car and opened the back door so the rest of us could pile out. Her eyes scanned the area, seeking out any potential threats. "Hurry."

Soon, Mona was out, and the six of us entered the restaurant while Tommy went to park the car.

Even though it was my second time here, I had almost forgotten what it looked like. The inside was dim with a large bar sitting on the left. It had displays of all of the wines and beers available for purchase. I took Mason's hand and headed straight to the hostess desk where a familiar young woman resided. Her wolf scent hit me once I got close.

She bowed her head at me. "Queen Elena." Her eyes then went to Mason. "King Mason." She pulled some menus out and glanced at the rest of the party. "Please follow me." She turned and headed toward a set of stairs.

Our group followed behind her, and she placed us right next to a window that overlooked Central Park. It was near the same table as last time. "Here you go." She placed the menus on the table in front of the four chairs. "Is there anything else I can get you right away?" Her gaze was directly on me.

"We have seven tonight." My guards needed a place to sit as well.

"No. No you don't." Kassie moved so she was sitting at a table next to us, and Mona sat at the table behind us. "We aren't eating, and we are separating to keep an eye out. Tommy will be watching the back door to this place as well."

"But ..." I hated that they wouldn't be eating with us.

"My Queen and King." Matteo appeared at the steps and hurried over to us. His golden eyes shone even more in the dim light and contrasted starkly against his dark olive skin. He had to be at least in his fifties. His eyes then went to Louis and Ella. "And of course my prince and ..." A smile played at the corner of his lips. "Dare I say his mate?"

"I may be his mate, but I have a name." Ella arched her eyebrow and turned to face him. "And it's Ella."

"Yes, of course." He smiled and nodded his head at her. "It's nice to see you again, Ella. Hopefully, this time, it'll be an altogether different experience." He then turned his focus back on me. "I'm glad you were able to make it this time."

"Me too." And that wasn't an understatement.

"Well, let's get your order started. What do you all want to drink? I can get that while you look over the menus." Matteo smiled.

We all quickly ordered and soon were alone at the table.

"I'm going to run to the bathroom." I stood, and both Kassie's and Mona's eyes landed immediately on me. "I'll be right back."

"Let me go clear the area first." Kassie stood and glanced at Mona. "I'll be right back."

"Should I go with her?" Ella stood right across from me.

"It wouldn't hurt." Mona turned her head from side to

side, keeping track of everything going on around us. Her phone dinged, and she pulled it from her pocket. "Kassie says it's clear."

"Come on, girl." Ella looped her arm through mine before we headed down the stairs to the bathroom. Kassie stood at the door and nodded as we entered.

I went straight to the counter.

"Hey, I thought you needed to use the bathroom?" Ella tilted her head and walked over to stand beside me.

"No, I just needed a minute." It took till now to realize how freaked out my guards were. Granted, I knew they were concerned, but not to this level. "It feels like I can't breathe."

"Girl, please." Ella reached over and ran her fingers through my hair. "You're probably the strongest person I'll ever meet. It's okay to feel overwhelmed every now and then."

"Thanks." She was trying to comfort me, but damn. . . There wasn't much more I could do right now. I had to get my shit together.

"How about I head out and give you a minute alone?" Ella smiled at me.

"Sounds good." I needed a minute.

"All right. Kassie and I will be right outside." She walked out the door. Once I was alone, I took a deep breath.

I turned the water on and thought about splashing it on my face. Dammit, I'd mess up my makeup. I turned it off and placed my hands on the countertop.

A stall door creaked open.

Spinning around, I found that all three doors were open and it didn't appear that anyone was in them. I glanced around, looking for an air vent or anything that would explain the noise. I took a step toward them, and there was no indication that anyone was in the bathroom. I had to be losing my mind.

When I turned back around to the mirror, my aunt was standing directly in front of me.

"What the ..."

Her makeup was dramatic as always; she wore way too much, and it looked thick and heavy. Every time I saw her while growing up, I'd always thought she looked like a lady of the night, but now she looked ... unhinged.

"Well, well, well." She tapped her pointer finger to her lips, and her dark black eyes sized me up and down.

If she thought I would stay here without yelling for my guards, she was damn crazy. I opened my mouth, which made her growl.

"If you scream, Tommy will die." She giggled like a maniac. "Honestly, I hated that bastard, so it wouldn't be much of a loss. The only thing he was ever good for was loyalty, and look where that got us."

Mason, my aunt is in the bathroom with me. She told me not to scream, but that didn't mean I couldn't alert my mate. *She's threatening Tommy, so don't make a scene. I think Richard must be out there with him.* "How did you get in here?" I had been alone; the bathroom was empty. This didn't make any sense.

"Wouldn't you love to know?" She glanced up at the ceiling and placed her hand on her heart. "This is what makes it even more fun."

"At least, one of us is enjoying herself."

"Oh, and boy am I." She chuckled as someone tried opening the door to the bathroom.

"They are way too clingy with you." Debra rolled her eyes and huffed. "But don't worry, we still have time to talk."

"I'm not interested." I turned and took a few steps toward the door.

"I wouldn't be so quick to dismiss me ... Queen." She made the word sound dirty. "I had told Darren that we needed to ensure you were dead, but he didn't listen to me."

"Obviously, you want something." She had to have had a witch spell her or something, but who the hell would do that? Supernatural races usually tried not to cause problems with other races, especially wolves since it was our core responsibility to maintain balance.

"Of course I do." She huffed and waved me off. "If you want this all to end, all you need to do is declare Richard as King and resign from your pitiful attempt as Queen."

"Are you being serious right now?" I needed whatever she was smoking.

We can't get in. Mason growled through the bond. *What does she want?*

If I could turn off a bond, then maybe I could open it up more so he could hear everything I could. I tugged deep on it and attempted to push it out.

"Look, I was against coming here and even giving you an option." Debra stomped her foot like a child. "I told them it was useless, but apparently we had to try. So here I am," she said as she waved her hand dramatically over her body, "trying."

"That's so nice of you." A nagging feeling pulled at me. I had to be prepared for anything.

"If you don't bow out as Queen, then we'll have to take the crown from you." Debra smirked, and her dark eyes filled with hate. "Obviously, I'm leaning toward the alternative."

"What did I ever do to make you hate me?" This is what I didn't understand. This woman had been a part of my life as I grew up. What did a six-year-old ever do to warrant so much hate?

"It's not about you, stupid girl!" She huffed and placed her hands on her hips. "It's about the position you hold. If we kill you or if you renounce yourself, Richard becomes the legit heir. It all works out."

"I refuse to let you pervert the monarchy." Did she honestly think I'd just walk away, knowing what type of people they truly are? "I figured out why Darren didn't visit the packs. They'd have known he wasn't king when they weren't able to submit to him."

"Maybe you aren't as stupid as we hoped." She shook her head and huffed. "But Darren was a much better leader than you could ever be. He died for no reason."

"You and he killed my parents. That wasn't a good reason?" Who the hell did she think she was?

Don't get her riled up. Mason growled, and the door began jerking again as he tried to open it. *She's insane, much like that Gabby woman.*

I'd never thought of it that way before, but he was right. "I won't step down. So bring the best you got."

She laughed so hard she clutched her side. "That's what I had hoped you would say." And then she disappeared from right in front of me.

It confirmed everything. She had someone with magic helping her. I backed up to the door, refusing to turn my back on the last place I'd seen her. When I got to the door, I opened it easily and found everyone standing there, even Matteo.

Mason grabbed me as Kassie burst into the bathroom, looking for her.

"What in the hell happened?" Ella's eyes were wide, and

she grabbed my arm. "Both Kassie and I made sure we were alone in there."

"There was a noise, and I turned to check it out. When I turned back around, she was there." I took in a deep breath and placed my head on Mason's chest.

"I already told them what was said." Mason pulled back and looked into my eyes. "We're going home now."

"Tommy was already guarding outside, so he's getting the car." Mona stood in front of me, making it so she and Mason surrounded me. Both of their bodies were tense and on high alert.

"Queen Elena, I'm so sorry." Matteo's face was pale, and he clutched his chest.

"It's not your fault. It could have happened anywhere." That was the thing; I wasn't sure if I'd be any safer at home.

CHAPTER FIVE

AS WE ARRIVED BACK HOME, my body felt lethargic. Now that the adrenaline had worn off, I was ready to head to bed. We wound up asking Matteo to pack up our food so we could take it home after what happened.

Are you okay? Mason slid from the Suburban and lifted his hand to help me crawl out on his side.

I'm just tired. I may just go to bed. Just thinking about eating almost made me want to vomit. I placed my hand in his, letting him help me from the vehicle.

You need to eat a little something. He kissed my forehead when I stepped onto the ground.

Ella, Louis, and Mona scrambled out the other side of the car. Pretty soon, all seven of us were climbing the front steps.

"I'm starving." Ella carried two bags full of food into the kitchen and laid them on the large island's light granite countertop. She began pulling out the containers of food. Each one had a name labeled on it. "Look at Matteo go. There's absolutely no question which person it belongs to."

"Were you trying to steal mine?" Louis grabbed the one with his name on it and turned so she couldn't reach it.

"Hey, what's yours is mine, and I want half." Ella pulled out a plastic fork, waving it in his direction.

Normally, I'd find all of this funny, but right now, I only wanted to sleep. I spun around, trying to sneak out, when Mason caught my waist.

"Just eat a little, and then I'll leave you alone." Mason reached over and picked up the container that had my name written on it.

"Listen to arm candy." Kassie entered the kitchen and scanned the entire room. "We had some guards sent here to do a thorough check before we arrived. Everything appears safe."

"It also did in the bathroom." Ella marched over to the large rectangular kitchen table and sat in the chair on the end. "I'm telling you there was no sign of anyone in that bathroom. I wouldn't have left her otherwise."

"And if anyone is to blame, it's me." Kassie frowned. "I cleared it before Elena and Ella ever went in."

"No one is blaming anyone." Louis sat next to Ella and opened his container, nudging it toward her. "Here, eat your feelings."

"If I wasn't so hungry, I'd smack you right now." She picked up her fork and stabbed his chicken parmesan.

I headed over to the light gray cabinets and pulled out a plate. I had a feeling I wouldn't be eating most of it.

"From here on out, Elena doesn't get left alone." Kassie grabbed her food, joining both Ella and Louis at the table. "If she breathes funny, we better know."

Oh, great. This was going to be fun. "Someone can't be with me twenty-four-seven." Please God, don't let someone be with me all the time. There are some things I want to do alone.

I joined everyone at the table, sitting right across from Ella.

Mason opened my chicken fettuccine and dumped half of it onto my plate.

"You said a little bit." I took my fork and stabbed the offending noodles. "This is not a little bit."

"By shifter standards, it is." Mona laughed as she and Tommy entered the kitchen and went to the island to get their own food.

"And here I thought, being Queen, you got to tell everyone else what to do." Ella moaned as she took a bite. "Now, I'm not quite as jealous anymore."

"Oh, that's so sweet." Louis leaned over and kissed her cheek. "Being royal actually means you have everyone telling you what to do. Sometimes even from your own pack members."

"Now, that isn't an understatement." There were times when it got overwhelming. Like right now.

"It's only because we love you." Mona winked at me.

"I get it. Still doesn't mean it's not hard." I took a bite of my food and it was good, but there was an odd taste to it. Sort of bitter. It was probably because my stomach was so messed up. I forced another bite into my mouth.

It wasn't long before I'd cleaned my plate and stood. "I did what you asked, and now I just want to go to bed."

"Okay, let's go." Mason stood and took a large drink of water.

"Don't worry. I'll clean this up." Mona nodded at him. "She looks exhausted. You two go rest."

"And when she says rest, she means sleep." Ella lifted

her finger and wagged it from side to side. "That doesn't mean sexy time."

"Now I might have to do it just because you said that." Mason glared at her.

"You should know better." Louis chuckled as he threw an arm around her shoulders.

"They both like to rag on each other." Tommy shook his head. "They'll never change."

"I don't like it when people figure out our secrets." Ella frowned and pouted.

"Hate to tell you, blondie." Kassie rolled her eyes. "It's not a secret."

Come on, let's get you to bed. Mason took my hand and tugged me toward the den. "Good night, everyone."

They all mumbled, "Good night," in return.

After passing through the den, we made our way back into our bedroom. It was a huge room holding a large sturdy bed with chestnut wooden frames. Not even bothering to remove my clothing, I crawled right in between the soft purple sheets.

Mason removed his suit pants and button-down shirt before crawling into bed next to me in only his underwear.

Normally, I'd be all over him, but tonight, I felt defeated. Not only did I not know who was targeting me, but my aunt had caught me completely off guard. To be honest with myself, I was more pissed that her words still hurt despite everything they'd done. Like, how did that hag still have power over me?

Stop beating yourself up. Mason pulled me against his chest, holding me tight.

How does it still hurt? I felt like I was that six-year-old girl I used to be, who realized some of her family members wanted her dead. *It's stupid.*

When you love, you love with all your heart. Mason kissed the back of my head. *Despite everything, you still love them. You grew up with them as your family and didn't realize the hurt they were going to try to inflict upon you. You let them in, and whether you like it or not, they still have a piece of you. They always will. That's one damn reason why you're so amazing. It's not a flaw; it's something beautiful.*

It doesn't feel so beautiful right now. My eyes grew heavy, and I welcomed sleep. I needed to turn my brain off even if it was only for a few hours.

It is. I love you.

His words were what I drifted off too.

"Elena." An unfamiliar scream woke me from my sleep.

I sat straight up and looked around. It took a second for everything to register. There was a bright light and then nothing. It was the exact same place I'd seen my parents when I'd almost died. "Mom? Dad?"

I heard a rustling, and soon they were in front of me. There was a wolf in front of them, baring its teeth.

"Haven't you done enough?" My dad's normal, composed face was lined with worry, and his eyes were filled with hurt. His body sagged in a way I'd never seen before.

"Stop. Don't hurt him." It took a second, but the midnight black fur registered. That wolf was my uncle. How was he now able to torment my parents?

Even though I was standing right there, no one turned toward me. It was as if no one could hear me.

My uncle shifted back into his human form and, thank

God, he had clothes on. This had to be some sort of dream; otherwise, none of this was making sense.

"Did you really think that Elena would win?" My uncle's blue eyes that matched both mine and my dad's shone with excitement. "Richard and Debra are already making plans to right the wrongs that had been done to us by both family and fate. You were never meant to be king."

"That's not true, and you know it," Dad said the words low and deep.

"Then why don't we fight for the title?" Darren laughed.

"It's not like it would change anything now." Mom took a step toward Darren, lifting her hands in the air. "We're all dead. That wouldn't resolve anything."

"It sounds like your mate doesn't think you can win." Darren laughed and took another menacing step toward them. "So it proves even more that I'm the one on top."

My dad stepped away from her.

"Corey, what are you doing?" Mom's mouth dropped open as realization dawned on her. "You can't be serious."

"Of course I am." Dad shook his head and glared at his brother. "He won't ever let this go. I have no idea why."

"You definitely know," Darren growled and took another step, closing the distance between them. "You had to take Gabby from me and then abandon her. I thought maybe we could reconnect, but she was still obsessed with you."

"I never knew you were interested in her. Besides, I'd found my mate." Dad threw his hands in the air. "If I could do it all over again, I would. That woman became the biggest pain in my ass."

"See, you didn't deserve her, just like you didn't deserve the crown." His hands clenched into fists.

"This doesn't make sense." Mom shook her head, making

her long red hair bounce from side to side. "You married Debra. Wasn't she your mate?"

"Hell, no." Darren wrinkled his nose as if the thought alone disgusted him. "We were just on the same page. She helped orchestrate the whole thing."

"You tried killing my daughter again." Dad pointed his finger toward Darren. "I'm tired of you taking out your anger on people I love."

"That was the point." Darren shifted back into his wolf and lunged for Dad's neck.

No. He couldn't hurt them again. I tried running toward them, but with each step, I discovered I didn't make any progress. The same distance between us was maintained despite my perceived forward motion. It didn't make any sense.

Dad growled and pushed his brother off him. "Stay back." Dad's words were almost indecipherable as he changed into his wolf. Dark auburn hair sprouted along his body as he shifted to all fours.

"Corey, no." Mom's face twisted in horror.

Darren began pacing around him, making it known he was the predator. Dad spun around, making sure his back wasn't turned to him.

It only took a moment before Darren charged at Dad once more. He lowered his head as if he was going to steamroll him to God knows where.

As his head shoved into Dad's side, Dad flipped his body over Darren's, landing back on his feet.

A deep growl emanated from my uncle.

I tried charging forward again, but I couldn't gain any traction. I was stuck at this distance for whatever reason. It was as if I was only allowed to be a spectator.

Not wasting a second, Darren attacked once more. He

stood up on his back two legs and fell on top of Dad.

Dad tried standing back on his hind legs, but Darren bit into the back of his neck and hung on.

Blood pooled and ran down my dad's red fur. However, it almost blended in. The only difference was the fur sticking together, making it visibly wet.

How the hell was this possible? This was supposed to be the afterlife.

"No. Corey," Mom yelled and ran toward them.

Darren unlatched from my father and bared his blood-soaked teeth at her.

That distraction was enough for Dad to be able to drop and get out from under Darren, causing my uncle to fall to the ground.

Within seconds, Dad jumped on his brother's back and forced him to the ground. However, Dad's teeth never dug into his skin.

The black wolf thrashed underneath him, but my dad maintained control.

It wasn't long before my uncle shifted back into human form underneath him. Dad followed suit, still making sure that my uncle couldn't break free.

My uncle's shoulders began to shake as if he was crying.

Dad rolled his shoulders, and blood began seeping through his shirt. He was injured.

"Look, I'm sorry." Darren's voice sounded pained. "I never meant to hurt anyone."

"That's a stretch." Dad released his hold on Darren and allowed my uncle to stand.

"Okay, but I didn't realize how far I'd taken it." He lifted both hands in the air in surrender.

That was bullshit. He had really meant to take it that far. Dad couldn't be falling for this.

"Look, I get it." Dad lowered his hands, letting down his guard. "It's hard to live this life. I know. If I could've saved Elena from this, I would've, hands down."

"Corey, be careful." Mom took a step toward him with her hand outstretched. "Every time you give him another chance, he winds up ..."

Before Mom could even finish her sentence, Darren pulled out a dagger that looked similar to the one that had been impaled in Louis's arm. He reared back and stabbed my father in the chest.

"No," I yelled and ran toward Dad.

He crumpled before our eyes, and blood began trickling from his mouth. "How could you?"

"Because I don't love you." Darren's face spread into a cruel smile, and he laughed. "How many times do I have to show you?"

"Dad." I sat up, screaming with tears pouring down my face.

"Elena, shh." Mason sat next to me and wrapped his arms around me. "It's just a dream."

"But it couldn't be?" I glanced around the room, looking for my dad on the ground, bleeding out.

"You've been here the whole time." Mason pulled me hard into his chest.

"When I passed out at the vampire prince's house, I saw my parents. They said I should be dead, but destiny had things work out the way they should, and I didn't have a lot of time with them. What I just saw was happening at the same place." My breathing was ragged, and my heart raced. "Darren killed my dad."

"I know that." Mason rubbed my arms, trying to get me to calm down.

"No, you don't understand. He killed him again." Tears

burned my eyes, threatening to spill over. "He killed Dad in the afterlife."

"You can't die in the afterlife." Mason's low voice was comforting.

"Why would I dream that?" It made no sense. "It wasn't a normal dream. It felt like I was yanked there and made to watch something. Every time I stepped forward; they moved another step away. It was like I was walking in place."

"Did your aunt spray something in your face or something?" A protective growl laced his words.

"What? No." My body stilled. "But my food tasted funny. Do you think ..."

"Yeah, someone had to have messed with you." Mason's fingers tightened on my arm. "Why did you eat it if it tasted off?"

"I figured it was just my nerves." I wanted to add that he had been dead set on it but didn't want to chance him feeling responsible.

"This is getting worse by the minute." Mason's body tensed. "We'll figure out what we need to do in the morning. Right now, we need sleep."

He was right, but I was scared. "Do you think I'll dream it again?"

"No, they're playing mind games with you, and you broke the spell when you woke up." Mason shook his head and kissed my head. "You should be safe now."

"Okay." I was even more exhausted than I had been when I went to sleep. I lowered my body and cuddled into Mason's chest. I needed his protective arms around me even more. If they'd been wanting me to be afraid to sleep, they'd won. If they could get at me even in my head, what was next?

CHAPTER SIX

WHEN I WOKE up the next morning, I found the bed empty. If I didn't know better, I'd think I partied hard last night. My head was pounding; my heart was heavy, and I wanted to barf.

Forcing myself to crawl out of bed, I stood on shaky legs and grabbed my phone, putting it in the pocket of the jumpsuit. I glanced at the mirror and grimaced. I looked like I was on my deathbed. My hair was flat. My skin was pale, and there were dark circles under my eyes. I winced. I either looked sick or like I was on drugs. I wasn't sure which option was the best. I should probably take a shower and change, but I needed caffeine, like, now.

I walked into the den and heard Mason's voice coming from the kitchen. It was low and hushed. "They somehow got something in her food that made her have a nightmare last night." Something loud like his hand hitting the counter echoed into the den. "She had to watch her dad die all over again."

"Something isn't right." Kassie sounded concerned.

"This doesn't make any sense. I've never heard of a normal run-of-the-mill witch being able to do all this."

"We've got to figure out who it is." Mona sighed. "Tommy, do you have any ideas?"

"For the first time ever, I don't." His deep voice was even lower than normal. "It's like we're fighting the air around us. It has to be a witch practicing dark magic."

His words chilled me to the bone.

"You've got an eavesdropper." Ella walked out of the kitchen and pointed at me. "Oh, damn, girl ... Are you okay?"

"What's wrong?" Mason's voice tensed, and I heard his footsteps rushing toward me. As he stepped into the den, he paused. "Oh, baby." He hurried over to me and wrapped me in his arms. "Did you have any more bad dreams? I shouldn't have left you alone."

"No, I just need coffee." I didn't want him to feel like he had to be glued to my side. He may be my mate, but I liked having some air to breathe on my own at times.

"Okay." He wrapped an arm around my waist and tugged me into the kitchen. With his free hand, he pointed to the table. "Go on and sit down. I'll make it for you."

Now that was something I wasn't going to argue with. I was under the watchful eyes of my three main guards as I sat at the table.

"You look like shit." Kassie frowned at me. "If I didn't know any better, I'd think you were doing a walk of shame right now."

"Thanks. That makes me feel so much better." Sometimes it was better not to say anything at all. I already felt bad enough.

"Wow. Our little princess is grouchy." Mona chuckled even though her brown eyes were full of worry.

"She's coming off a magic high." Louis sat at the end of the table right across from me and shook his head with closed eyes. "I've seen this done to my brother once. He had a rendezvous with a witch and woke up the same way. She'd tried to spell him to get some secrets. Little did she know that he wasn't privy to the information."

"How long did it last?" I'd never felt like this before. Even as a kid, I had never gotten sick due to my shifter half.

"A day or two." Louis frowned. "So at least, the end is in sight."

"That's it. I'm not eating out again." At least, not until this whole thing was over.

"It's for the best." Tommy nodded his head. "We've got to figure out what the hell is going on. I've never felt useless like I do now."

"I think we're all feeling that way." It was as though, no matter what we tried to do, something attacked us without warning.

My cell phone rang, the noise piercing my head. "Oh, damn it."

"You don't have to answer that." Mason placed a cup of coffee on the table in front of me.

It would be nice to ignore it, but when I saw Xavier's name on the caller ID, I had to answer. When one of the main alphas from Chicago called, it wasn't usually a good thing. "Hello?"

"Queen Elena." It wasn't a question but more a statement of fact.

"Yes, is everything okay?" They normally didn't call randomly like this. We had weekly calls scheduled with the alphas in which we discussed everything.

"I'm not so sure." He cleared his throat and took a deep

breath. "I normally wouldn't feel inclined to call, but after you and your mate did so much for us, I can't not."

My heart dropped. This was going to be bad. "I appreciate it so much. What seems to be the issue?"

"There are some rumblings that some alphas are beginning to conspire to take the crown from you."

"What?" I put the phone on the table and hit SPEAKER. I didn't want to have to repeat this to everyone. "I just put you on speaker. Mason and my close circle are near. It'll make this talk go much smoother."

"Of course, My Queen." He cleared his throat. "Even though you and the king have only been in place for a few months, there is a group of alphas that feel neglected and think that you show favoritism."

"That's bullshit," Mason growled.

"I know. We've informed them of that, but they think it's because we've been visited." He paused. "Your cousin is down there. They're backing him for the crown."

At some point, I had to stop being surprised. "Of course, he is."

"He's promising them things."

"That son of a bitch is going down." Mason placed his hands on my shoulders and began kneading.

"What cities are we talking about?" There was no telling who all were involved.

"Right now, we're talking about Nashville and Atlanta."

Of course, the bigger cities south of us. "Thank you for letting me know." At least, this time we might be ahead of the curve.

"It's an honor." His voice lowered. "If you need any additional support, please don't hesitate to reach out."

"Thank you." I pressed END and grabbed the coffee,

taking a sip. Mason had fixed it perfectly with just the right amount of cream and sugar. "Can this get any worse?"

"Well, maybe we can try to pretend we don't know." Ella entered the kitchen and pursed her lips. "They probably don't know that he's called you."

"That's a good point." Louis frowned. "But you need to act on it quickly. The longer he puts those thoughts in their heads, the harder it's going to be to prove otherwise."

"Hopefully, they'll think they have more time to brainwash the packs." Mason nodded his head but leaned over, kissing the top of my head. "But we can wait until you're better."

No, we couldn't. "I love you for that, but, Kassie, please call the pilot, and get us scheduled to leave here in the next two hours."

"Elena." Mason's voice was low, laced with warning.

Fuck that. The longer we waited, the more they could manipulate and mess with me. "There's a bed on the new plane. I'll rest there. It won't make much of a difference anyway." The guards had wanted a new plane with more state of the art security features.

"She's right." Louis forced a sad smile. "The longer you wait, the worse it'll be."

"But she's not well." Mason glanced at Kassie. "Tell them."

"There isn't a right answer." She stood from her spot and took a deep breath. "I'll go make the arrangements."

The last thing I needed was another fight between Mason and me. I stood and turned around to face him. "I promise to sleep on the plane." I was barely able to stand for long; I needed the rest. "And when we get there, you'll be by my side."

His shoulders loosened, and he chewed on his bottom lip. "I don't like this."

"But she's right, and you know it." Ella pointed at her brother. "So let's get ready to go."

"Who said you two are going?" Mona arched an eyebrow and sat back in her seat.

Tommy grinned from ear to ear. "It's rare I get to see this side of her."

"Of course, we're going. We're the fabulous four." Ella shook her head like it was common knowledge.

"No, not this time." The last time we went somewhere, Alec, Mason's best friend, was captured by the vampire prince and held hostage. We almost didn't get him back alive. "I can't deal with anyone else I love getting injured. Just stay here and behave."

"But ..." Ella pouted.

"She's right." Louis turned to her.

"If you say that one more time, I may slap you." Ella leaned forward with a sneer.

"I'll line up some other guards, and we'll get on our way." Tommy stood, and as he headed out the door, Kassie popped her head in.

"They'll be ready in two hours, let's get packing and move." Kassie waved us on. "We're stopping at the Atlanta hub first since it's the busiest and most influential."

That made the most sense. "Okay, let me go at least attempt to look presentable."

"I'm not being left behind." Ella crossed her arms and stood firm. "Every time we split up, something happens to one of us. We're going."

I didn't have the energy to fight. "Fine."

"Woot." She lifted both arms up in the air.

"Come on." Mason took my hand and tugged me to the door.

Within a few seconds, we were back in the bedroom. "You need to shower and lie down. I'll get everything packed and will stay close in case you need me."

That wasn't something I wanted to argue with. I quickly took a shower and got myself at least somewhat presentable. Then, I climbed into bed while listening to the comforting sounds of him near and drifted to sleep.

ARMS SLIPPED underneath my neck and my knees, picking me up from the bed. My eyelids began to flutter, but the comforting, earthy scent of Mason surrounded me. I snuggled into his chest some more and could hear his heartbeat pounding in my ear.

"Is it time yet?" I took a deep breath and opened my eyes as we were breezing through the den.

"Yes, everyone is in the car, waiting for us." He smiled at me. "Some of your color is coming back."

Now that he mentioned it, I didn't feel quite as horrid any longer. "I feel a little better."

"Good."

When we made it to the garage, Kassie was holding the door open for us.

Mason placed me gently on the ground, and I climbed in to sit in my usual spot behind the driver. Within seconds, we were pulling out of the garage.

"Have you heard any updates?" There was no telling what I might've missed while napping.

"No, not really." Tommy glanced in the rearview mirror

at me. "Which is a good thing. They aren't making waves yet."

"We should've already visited more places." I hated that I'd let them down so much.

"Between the vampire attacks? Or when you had to heal from a near-death injury? Or the holidays? Or wait, when we had to plan a coronation for Mason?" Ella piped up from the back seat in her usual spot in the middle. "I mean, we had so much free time that I could see where we might beat ourselves up over it."

"Don't be an ass." Mason turned around and glared at his sister.

"No, she's right." There had been a lot going on. It's not like I was being Darren and purposely neglecting them. I couldn't think of any reasons why they'd be willing to follow Richard after the way his father had reigned.

"Still could be nicer about it," he grumbled as he faced forward again.

"Oh, did I hurt your feelings?" Ella snorted in the back seat.

"Ella." Even Louis's low tone held a warning.

"Right now, we need to focus on getting there and then figuring everything out." We had to work through things one at a time.

It wasn't long before we were pulling up to the airport. Tommy stopped in front of the entrance.

Kassie jumped out and scanned the area. She paused before coming over and opening our door. "Let's get out."

The six of us exited the vehicle while some people were unloading our bags. When Tommy drove off to find a parking space, we walked inside.

As usual, Kassie was in front, scanning everything, and

Mona was guarding the back. When we entered the building, everyone seemed to get even more tense.

It was more crowded than usual, and Kassie stayed close to us as we swerved through the crowd and headed to our gate.

A chill ran down my back. I glanced around and couldn't find anything or anyone unusual standing out.

Are you okay? Mason's concerned voice filled my head.

I don't know. Something feels off. A few people had looked our way, but that was nothing out of the ordinary. *Do you feel it?*

No, but that means something is definitely wrong. He stepped closer to me and took my hand. *Whoever it is likes only you being aware.*

That sounded about right. *Let's just get on the plane.* I was hoping it was due to me not feeling the best and surrounded by all of these people. Maybe I was being paranoid.

As we entered the plane, some of the edginess had worn off. *The feeling has gone away.*

Thank God. Mason took my hand and led me toward the bedroom at the very back of the plane.

I stopped, making Mason pause. "Do one of you mind getting me an outfit before we leave?" I wanted to make sure I at least looked somewhat put together when we landed.

"Yeah, I'll grab something." Mona headed off the plane, passing Tommy as he climbed on board.

Tommy made his way to the cockpit. "How much longer until we take off?" His voice was tense and direct.

"Once the guard gets back on the plane." The pilot sounded almost terrified of Tommy.

"Perfect." He nodded at the captain and headed toward us. "Do I need to check anything?"

"Nope, I already checked the cabin." Kassie glanced at Mason. "Go back there with her. We aren't leaving her alone."

"I planned to."

"Let her sleep though." Ella sat on one of the couches that had a drawer next to it, and she was facing a television. "I don't want to hear anything, and she still appears as if she's at death's door."

"Sometimes, you can be quiet." Louis smiled at her adoringly but shook his head.

"Nah, it's part of my charm." Ella winked at him as she pulled some beef jerky out of the drawer.

"What charm?" Mason reached over and snatched the bag she had just pulled out.

"Hey, that's mine." Ella pouted and held her hand open, waiting for him to give it back.

"It's for Elena." He took my hand, and together we began heading to the back.

"Then it's fine, but you better not have one morsel," Ella yelled at him.

Normally, they would crack me up, but I still had a huge headache and wished they'd be quiet.

Mona jogged back onto the plane and tossed Mason a small duffle bag. "Here are the extra sets of clothes you packed. She should be good to go."

"Thank you." I didn't know what I'd do without every single one of these people in my life.

Mason opened the door to the bedroom, and I sat on the bed to open the bag, wondering what they had packed for me. Thankfully, it was a pair of jeans and a shirt. It might not be the most regal of attire, but they knew I'd want to be comfortable. Just as I set the bag on the floor, a flash of light caught my eye.

My body tensed as I leaned over and dug through my bag. My hand hit something cool and smooth. I pulled it out from the bag, and just like twice before, I found a small sphere-shaped stone, red and black mixed together with the double infinity sign.

"What's that?" Mason's voice sounded deep and raspy.

He already knew what it was. "It's another marble."

"Of course it is." He stepped next to me and stared at it. "Do you know what that symbol means?"

"Revenge." Granted, I already knew that was what Debra and Richard wanted, but how did they manage to sneak it into this bag? That's the part that scared me the most.

CHAPTER SEVEN

MY HEART THUDDED in my chest. "Do you think something is wrong with our plane?" Would someone be desperate enough to want me dead that they'd take the whole plane down?

"I don't know." He took the marble from my hand and closed his eyes. "This is getting to be too much."

"At some point, we have to get a reprieve, right?" At least, I sure hoped so. I spun around and opened the door. We needed to take care of this before we took off.

"What's wrong?" Mona's eyes landed on mine immediately. "You're supposed to be resting."

"Someone left me another present in my bag." I glanced at Kassie and Tommy. "There's another marble, this time with the double infinity sign."

"Revenge." Kassie jumped to her feet. "We need to get off of the plane immediately and make sure everything is okay."

"What if that's what they want?" Mason ran his hands through his hair. "This could go so many ways."

"It's probably nothing." Ella waved her hand as if she was brushing it off. "They're purposely riling you up."

"Well, someone is going to check the plane, at least." Tommy stood, headed toward the pilot's door, and banged on it.

"I'm with Ella." Louis tensed and scanned the inside of the plane as if he was going to see something we couldn't. "They're playing mind games. As of now, they haven't gone out of the way to hurt you themselves, not directly."

"Which is exactly their motive," Kassie growled and paced in a circle. "It was Gabby who was supposed to kill her, then they made her watch her dad die again, so by rigging the plane, it's once again set up so they're not directly hurting her."

"That's one way of thinking about it, but Ella might not be wrong." Mona tapped her finger on her lips.

Soon, the pilot hurried out of the cabin and ran down the steps to the ground.

Tommy appeared with a frown set deep on his face. "He's going to make sure everything mechanical gets checked over once more."

"Okay, good." Kassie stopped for a second and took a deep breath. "Now, what were you saying?"

"Think about it." Mona tapped her foot on the ground. "Yes, they left a knife with Gabby, but they also didn't know that Elena would come with her security crew, if at all. And her aunt didn't try anything in the bathroom with her despite the door being magically sealed shut, and with the dream, she was never in danger of truly being harmed."

"They are definitely fucking with her mind." Mason pulled me into his arms and took a deep breath. *Maybe we shouldn't go.*

We have to. I wasn't thrilled about the prospect either,

but damn ... there were actual packs whispering about challenging my throne. *They win either way. Either I go and deal with the mess they've created for us, or I stay safe, and they bring the war to me. There isn't a way of winning in this.*

One day, we're getting away and spending time enjoying each other. No worries or anything. Mason's strong arms wrapped around me.

That sounds perfect. The thought of him and me at a beach or, hell, even a mountain retreat so we could relax and be a part of nature sounded more than exquisite.

"See, I can get into a stalker's head." Ella sat straight up in the seat and rolled her shoulders back.

"That's not necessarily a good thing." Kassie shook her head at her.

"Actually, it is." Louis wrapped his arm around his mate, pulling her flush against his side. "It's a strategic advantage to get into your opponent's mind. I'd think guards would need to be able to see things like this too."

"Maybe if there weren't three people going after her at all times." Kassie sighed as the pilot clambered back into the aircraft.

"Everything is locked and loaded." He appeared to be around the same age as Tommy and smelled of wolf. "I have no reservations about taking off."

All six sets of eyes stared at both Mason and me. They were waiting for us to give the order.

You think we should go? Mason's voice was strained, but he already knew the answer.

Yes. I do. We have to get there, and the longer it takes, the worse it'll be.

"Let's go. Worse case, we'll use the parachutes or whatever in here." He tugged me toward the bedroom again.

"She's going to rest. Let me know if anyone needs us or if something goes wrong."

Tommy nodded his head. "Yes, my King."

"All right. I'll get us on the runway." The pilot went back into his cockpit.

As we entered the back bedroom again, I took a deep breath. It was only a double bed with cream-colored sheets. The size made it hard for both Mason and me to fit, but I was always up for the challenge, and it was nice having a room to ourselves.

He placed the marble back in my bag and sighed. "Will things ever settle down?"

"I think so." I had to believe that. I couldn't imagine the rest of our lives being this crazy. "You don't regret this, do you?"

"Hell no." He moved to lie on the bed, sliding over against the wall. He spread his arms, waiting for me to cuddle into him. "Of course not."

"Being with me isn't easy, I know." I crawled into his arms and placed my head on his chest. I took a deep breath, feeling right at home.

"And being without you would be impossible." He kissed the top of my head as I closed my eyes.

We lay in silence as I listened to his heartbeat and breathing which calmed my racing heart. The plane began to speed up for takeoff, and soon we were soaring into the sky.

After several long minutes, I gave up on trying to sleep. Despite how hard I tried, my brain wouldn't shut off. *Are you awake?*

Nope, but you should be sleeping. He began to rub his fingers along my back.

I can't shut it off. Obviously, Debra and Richard are

doing most of this, but someone had to help orchestrate it. Who the hell could it be? Was it someone that I'd wronged or maybe my parents had? There were so many possibilities it made me dizzy.

Your guess is as good as mine. He kissed my forehead. *But we'll figure it out. They'll mess up, and we'll catch a break.*

There's no telling what Richard has said to the alphas. We had no clue what we were walking into other than knowing that the alphas and their packs were turning on me for some reason. It had to be at least good or convincing in order for them to believe my cousin after the way his father had treated everyone.

He must be convincing them somehow. His arms tensed around me. *But, you're supposed to be resting.*

Well, I can't stop my mind from running. I pulled back and looked into his eyes. *I could think of one way, though, of shutting it off.*

Oh, really now. He arched an eyebrow and lowered his head. *How exactly is that?*

Instead of words, I decided it'd be better to show him. I pressed my lips against his and reveled in being completely surrounded by him.

I kind of like your idea. He deepened our kiss, making me dizzy.

A loud knock sounded on the door right before it opened. Ella popped her head in. "FYI, we can hear you all the way out here?"

"What the hell?" Mason leaned back and glared at his sister. "The door was locked."

She held up a bobby pin. "They made it easy to unlock in case of an emergency." She rolled her eyes.

"Really?" Now that she'd said it, that kind of made sense.

"Duh." She snorted as she took in my expression.

"Is this an emergency?" Mason growled the words in warning.

"Yeah, it really is." Ella placed her hands on her hips and glared. "The last thing that any of us wants to hear coming from in here are moans and groans. I was afraid the bed was about to squeak."

"We weren't moaning." Actually, I wasn't quite sure about that. For some reason, I thought the small room would be more soundproofed.

"Oh, you were." Ella pointed her finger at me. "It may be a new plane, but it's not sound proof."

I wanted to turn invisible right now. "Good to know."

There's no reason to be embarrassed. We'll pretend like she's not here. He lowered his head to mine, kissing me slow and sweet.

"I'm right here." Ella's voice raised an octave.

What are you trying to do? If he thought this was some sort of punishment for his sister, I was all for it.

She tried riling us up with her theatrics. His tongue skimmed my lips. *I figure we owe her a show.*

"Don't make me have to sit between you two." Ella took a few steps closer to us. "Because I will."

For the love of God. Mason pulled away and readjusted so I was against his chest. "There, Mom. We're behaving."

"Good." Ella sighed. "Because that could have gotten awkward like that one time you kissed my hand."

"You put it between our mouths." Mason's voice was low and annoyed. "Don't make it sound like I actively sought it out."

"Leave them alone, for God's sake." Louis chuckled. "They are now fully aware that we can hear them."

"We're resting, promise." Even though Ella was annoying as hell, she had some kind of charm. "You can even leave the door open."

"Okay, but one more sound, and I'll be taking his place." She winked at me as she turned around and skipped back to her seat.

Why did we bring her again? Mason growled in my ear.

Because she might have been more of a target otherwise. We had actually been torn on that decision.

Fine, but next time, I might be willing to take our chances. He growled.

"Noises," Ella called from the other room.

My shoulders shook with laughter. *I guess we better behave and actually try to take some kind of nap.*

When we landed, the Atlanta airport surprised me, it was the largest airport I'd ever been in. Even the private area was packed.

As we climbed from the aircraft, it felt nice to place my feet on solid ground after our initial scare. "Do we have vehicles and a hotel lined up?"

"Of course we do." Mona grinned as she caught up to me. "Do you think this is our first rodeo?"

"Let me guess—Suburbans?" Ella rolled her eyes as she shook her head.

"Of course." Tommy laughed as his hand brushed against Kassie's.

"And we'll be staying at the Four Seasons." Kassie

noticed my glance and stepped away from Tommy. "I'm just glad nothing happened on the flight. I'd been worried."

"I'm not sure if it's much better." Louis frowned and shook his head. "Head games can be more brutal and tragic than physical trauma."

He was right on that. Watching my dad die all over again continued to haunt me. It didn't even matter that it was only a dream.

"Well, once we figure out who it is, we'll level the playing field." There was a darkness to Mason's tone.

We entered the airport and hurried through the crowd.

"Tommy and Mona are going to go ahead and take you to the hotel while I stay behind and load up the second vehicle." Kassie motioned to the two Chevys ahead.

"Someone needs to be with you." I hated to leave her alone. "What if something happens?"

"It won't." Kassie's voice was tense.

"There's got to be a way we can all stay together." If we left and she got hurt or worse, I wouldn't be able to live with myself.

"Elena is right." Mason took my hand and stepped closer to me. "We'll all leave together."

Kassie's eyes narrowed. "But ..."

"You heard them." Tommy's tone was rigid. "And I agree. We can get them settled into the first vehicle, and Mona can keep watch. It'll be easier to take one Suburban anyway."

"But we said two." Anger flared in her eyes.

"It's not safe." Mona's calming voice interjected. "It's better with larger numbers."

"Fine." She hurried over to the black vehicle in front and opened the trunk. "Get those four inside now."

I hated how each one of us felt stressed at this moment.

Mona hurried to the car door as Tommy kept an extra eye out for anything out of place. I rushed into the car so the other three could climb in right after.

"Was it always like this when your dad ruled?" Louis asked as he brushed by me on the way to his normal seat in the back.

"Not as far as I can remember. His reign was expected, and it was mapped out seamlessly with little to no backlash." Dad had told me that growing up in the spotlight always helped the transition into the crown easier if done correctly. However, I didn't get to have that privilege. "Granted, there were things that came up, but nothing like this."

"It's even further proof that your uncle messed everything up." Ella sat next to Louis and placed her head on his shoulder. "It appears he didn't even do the job as needed."

Two men put our four bags into the back of the Suburban and then sealed it up. Mason's side door opened, and Mona began crawling through to the back.

"That went faster than expected." She sat in the back next to Ella and scanned our surroundings as Kassie and Tommy climbed into the car.

"It's only twenty minutes from here." Tommy shifted the car into DRIVE and merged with the traffic.

The sun was setting, and it hit me that it was slightly past six. "It's too late to try to schedule a meeting." I pulled my phone from my pocket and scrolled through my contacts. "I'm going to call them and schedule something for in the morning."

"Whatever we need to do." Mason nodded at me and reached over to brush his fingertips on my arm.

"Okay." I took a deep breath and pulled up Brent, the

alpha for Atlanta, in my contacts and pressed CALL. The line rang, and I felt my stomach drop.

Right when I thought I'd be sent to voicemail, someone answered.

"Hello?" His voice was deep and strong.

"Brent, hi." I took a deep breath. I had to be tough. "This is Elena. Sorry for such short notice, but we've landed at the airport a few minutes ago and plan to stay a few days."

"Have you really?" His voice was laced with humor. "After almost three months, you've finally decided to grace us with your presence?"

He wasn't going to give me any slack. "I do apologize for the length of delay, but between our coronations, the holidays, and some other very pressing matters arising, this was our first opportunity."

"It's odd that you find time now." He huffed. "So are you demanding that I meet you now? Is that what this is about?"

He was direct. That, at least, showed where we stood with him. "Of course not. I figure you're just as busy as anyone. I was hoping we might meet for breakfast. Maybe you could come join us in the morning at the Four Seasons?"

"Only if we meet downstairs in the main restaurant." He chuckled.

He was dictating to me what we were going to do and seeing how far he could go. I should push back, but then he might refuse to meet at all. I had to choose my battles. "Fine. Does nine work for you?"

"I'll be there." He paused for a moment. "Good night." Then, the phone line went dead.

He's testing us already. Mason reached over and intertwined his fingers with mine. *I don't like it.*

Me neither. Only tomorrow would tell whether we had another enemy to add to our list.

CHAPTER EIGHT

WE PULLED up to a large building in the heart of Atlanta, Georgia. There was a castle-like feel to the facade with five American flags on display, and it was attached to a huge, more modern building.

"Here we are," Tommy said as he pulled into the small, arch drive in front. "Let's get them inside so we can all get settled."

"On it." Kassie opened the door and began scanning the area, looking for any looming threat nearby. One of the workers immediately headed in her direction, and she pointed to the back of the car. The person nodded his head and made his way over to us.

Tommy opened the driver's door and hurried to the back of the car, popping the trunk.

"Do you know where I should take the bags?" the hotel worker asked as he grabbed our luggage and put them on a cart that was nearby.

"The presidential suite." Tommy glanced in at Mona. "You guys can leave. Kassie gave the all-clear."

The worker glanced into the back as if trying to figure

out who we were but apparently knew better than to ask any questions.

He was probably at a loss as to why we were getting treated in such a manner.

I opened the door and climbed out with Mason and then Mona close behind me.

"I'm running inside to get the room keys. Kassie will stay out here and continue security sweeps." She rushed past Tommy and headed toward the front desk.

The rest of the crew got out, and soon we were all heading inside. Mason stood close to me on one side with Kassie on the other.

It appeared as if we were all on high alert after the aircraft scare. Luckily nothing horrible had happened, just a mind game.

When we walked into the huge lobby, it kind of surprised me that no matter how nice the hotel was, it had a similar feel to any other. Yes, it was nicer than the ones I used to stay at before becoming Queen: golden touches, nicer furniture, and a fancy chandelier. Except, it still had the same feel, a huge open area where we could see all the way to the back of the building.

Mona walked away from the front desk and nodded at our group. "Let's move. The elevator is over here."

We walked in the middle of two sets of large stairways that led to the second level. It was the same sort of style that we had back in the old NYC apartment where we used to live.

Following Kassie's lead, we turned toward the elevators.

Let me know if you smell or see anything weird. Mason held my hand even though he was so close to me that our arms brushed with every step.

Nothing seems out of sorts. At least, for now. The last

time we were at a hotel, his best friend Alec had gone missing courtesy of the vampire prince. It was a long, drawn-out process to save him. And even when we did, he had been so severely injured he still wasn't back to his old self.

As all seven of us crammed inside the elevator, Ella let out a huge breath. "Was it only me who was ready for something to jump out or grab one of us the entire way in?"

"Don't jinx us," Kassie snapped as she turned her head in Ella's direction. "We haven't made it to the room yet."

Mona reached over and ran the key over a scanner and pressed nineteen. "Calm down, everyone. Whoever it is wants us on edge. We'll be able to relax in a few minutes."

It wasn't long before we reached the presidential suite. The elevator doors opened to a large foyer that led straight into a huge living room.

"Stay here," Mona instructed the four of us while the guards checked every room.

"This is almost as big as our house back home." Ella snorted and shook her head. "It sometimes puts things into perspective how the rich people don't understand the common middle-class people."

"That's what makes them so unique." Louis pointed at Mason and me. "They know and understand."

"Yet, we've been focusing on the alphas that didn't understand." Maybe we'd handled everything wrong. Brent was one of the same alphas in question, and he wasn't a fan of ours. Granted, that probably had more to do with his self-worth. He was the alpha over Atlanta, one of the largest supernatural hubs in the world. It was the third-largest.

"That's how the game is played, unfortunately." Louis glanced around the place. "It's weird; I've always grown up in places like this. Yet, the place you all consider home feels more comfortable for me as well."

"Hate to break it down for you, buddy, but it's your home too." Ella arched an eyebrow. "You're my other half, which means it's a damn good thing you like it."

"Duly noted." He chuckled.

We need to be super careful here. Mason wrapped his arm around me, pulling me close. I could feel the tension in his whole body, and our bond was flooded with worry. *I can't let another bad thing happen to you.*

The same for you. I'll never forget what it was like right after we had completed our bond back home in South Carolina. The vampire prince had just found me, and I was working at the Flying Monkey, which was a trendy bar on the outskirts of town. I'd worked there as the dishwasher. Mason had come to do some of his college homework and keep an eye on me. Little did I know that Darren already had his cronies looking for me. They'd somehow knocked Mason out and abducted him for leverage. When I came out of the kitchen, all I had found was his books and cell phone. There was no trace of him anywhere in the bar.

"It's clear." Kassie walked back in with Tommy and Mona following behind her. "However, don't let your guard down. If anyone goes out on the balcony, for the love of God, come grab at least one of us."

"I promise." For so long, the three of them had been there for me. I hated seeing them so stressed out. Despite that, even when I gave Mona and Kassie an out for raising me, they'd insisted on maintaining their roles as guards. At least, we were paying them a salary now.

We entered the living room. It was an open floor plan connecting to the dining area. There was a large, gray, L-shaped couch in the middle with the back butting up against a thick glass wall.

There was a seventy-inch flat screen hung opposite the couch and a small sofa to the side.

"At least, we have time to watch a movie or something tonight." Ella yawned as she sat on the couch. "And it's surprisingly comfortable."

A ding alerted us to the elevator door opening, and the man from downstairs rolled in our luggage. "Let me know if you need anything."

"We're good. Thank you though." I smiled at him, just wanting to be alone.

"What are we going to do for dinner?" Ella huffed as she pulled her legs onto the couch and wrapped her arms around them. "I'm hungry."

After the day we'd all had, going out didn't sound like a great idea. "Why don't we order a pizza?" Even though I was hesitant to eat out, there wasn't any other option here. At least, I knew what nightmare inducing herbs tasted like after the other night.

"A pizza?" Ella arched her eyebrow. "That's only enough for me."

"You know what she means." Mason rolled his eyes as he sat on the other end of the couch and patted the seat beside him. "And that sounds great to me."

"Thank God." Kassie yawned and shook her head. "I don't think I'd be up for doing anything else today. It's been rough. Remember, if the food tastes funny, you don't eat it."

"You're not kidding," Mona said as she walked over and grabbed my and Mason's bag. "I can run down to the lobby and pick it up if someone will order it."

"And for the love of God, please make sure there are at least two pepperoni and sausage pizzas. Otherwise, Ella won't let me have any." Louis frowned even though his eyes seemed to flicker with mirth.

"Hey, I don't share food. Blame it on Mason." She pointed her finger at him. "He would eat food right off my plate."

Just now, everything felt almost normal. I headed over to Mason and sat next to him.

"Because you'd take the whole meal, all the servings Mom fixed." He wrapped his arm around me and leaned his head down to my ear. "Mom loves making meatloaf cupcakes. She says it's so much easier than a big glob so it reduces cooking time."

"Okay." I wasn't quite sure why he was telling me this.

"Ella runs into the kitchen to get her serving and takes all twelve." Mason narrowed his eyes at his sister. "Everything! Didn't even leave any for Mom."

"And she said I was a growing girl." Ella dropped her feet back to the ground and crossed her arms. "When are you going to stop throwing that in my face. Let it go. It was so last year."

"Sometimes, I wonder how we were mated to those two." Louis caught my eye and shook his head. "They aren't quite like anyone else I've ever met."

"Watch it, Luey!" She tilted her head and leaned back against the couch and threw one of the pillows at him.

"I hate that name," Louis growled. "Stop it."

"What would everyone like?" Tommy pulled his phone from his pocket. "I think food may help the atmosphere in this room."

Ella did get angry when she hadn't eaten. Maybe once we got the food here, she would calm down. That's what I was hoping for anyway. "I'm good with a pizza all the way."

"Same for me." Mason moved his arm down and took my

hand. He stood and tugged me in the direction Mona had walked. "Let's go get situated."

"Yeah, I may change into some pajamas." Climbing to my feet, I took a deep breath.

"Just ordered the food." Tommy placed his phone on the table and sat on the small couch across the way. "It'll be here in thirty minutes."

"Got it. We won't be long."

The wall on the far-left side of the living room ended, making a small hallway to the left of the room. We entered the hallway and walked past a half bath to a door directly in front of us. It was wide open, and when we entered the room, Mona was out on the balcony, looking around.

Her eyes met mine, and she headed back into the room. "I needed to make sure nothing looked or smelled funny out there."

"Thank you for doing that." I walked into the room and sat on the large king bed that was centered against the back wall. The cover was white and soft under my hands.

"All right, I'm going to go get Ella and Louis's room set up now." She grabbed the blinds and slid them shut so the balcony couldn't be seen. "There is an adjoining room they will be staying in."

"Where are you guys going to stay?"

"There is a pull-out couch in part of the sectional, and Tommy plans on sleeping on the couch. Despite how big the combined hotel rooms are, there are only two real bedrooms."

"But it's small." I hated the sacrifices they made.

"It's fine." She shrugged. "Worst case scenario, I'll take the couch."

"And Kassie and Tommy would sleep together?" I couldn't help the small smile that slipped through.

"What?" Mona's eyes widened, and she covered her mouth with her hand.

"Don't worry." Mason joined me on the bed and bumped his shoulder into mine. "We'd been suspicious all along."

"I didn't say anything." Mona rolled her eyes and laughed. "They think they're able to hide it, but more subtle things are beginning to show."

"But they hated each other." That's what I couldn't grasp. I remembered, when I was little, Kassie would constantly attack the poor man.

"There is a thin line between love and hate." Mona lifted her eyebrows and made her way to the door. "That saying is around for a very good reason."

As I watched her walk down the hall back to the others, a chill ran through me. That's the same thing I had said to Tommy just last week.

I'm glad we got here in one piece. Mason sighed and turned to examine my face.

That's when I realized there were dark circles under his eyes. That wasn't normal at all. *Were you that worried?*

I believed that everyone was right and that they wouldn't mess with the plane, but hell, what do I know. He lifted his hand and tucked a piece of my hair behind my ear. *The thought of losing you scares the shit out of me.*

I'm right here. I lifted my chin and kissed his lips ever so softly.

A small knock came at the door. "Hey, do you guys have a second?"

Every damn time. I should've closed and locked the door. Mason huffed.

"What's up?" I glanced at Louis, who scratched at the back of his neck.

"I feel awful doing this, but I have a bad feeling." He bit at his bottom lip. "Do you mind if I come in here for a second?"

"Of course not." I waved him into the room. "Are you okay?"

"Yeah, but I'm a little worried." He entered the room and glanced behind him. "Do you mind if I shut the door?"

"What the fuck do you want?" Mason's tone was tense. *He's acting strange, and his heart is racing. Nothing good can come of this.*

Mason's reaction startled me some, but I tried to contain it.

"I kind of deserve that." He took a deep breath and began pacing the room. "My dad is a wild card."

"Okay ..." I wasn't quite sure where he was going.

"By telling you this, I'm not sure if there will ever be a way for me to redeem myself in his eyes, but you two should know." He rubbed a hand down his face.

"Out with it." Mason's jaw clenched. "Or I'll beat it out of you."

Calm down. I understood he was upset. He'd been on edge all day, but we couldn't blow up. *He's your sister's mate, for God's sake. He's family.*

"No, look. I'm not quite sure how to say it, so I'm just going to put it out there." Louis took a deep breath and sighed. "My father helped your uncle kill your parents."

Out of everything that could be said, I hadn't expected this. "But ... why?"

Mason jumped to his feet and closed the distance between them. "And you're just telling us this now?"

"Look, I ..." Even before Louis could finish speaking, Mason reared back and punched him right in the jaw. Louis fell back into the wall and landed with a thud on the floor.

"What the hell is going on?" Kassie hollered from the living room.

Just as Louis grabbed his nose to pinch it, trying to keep the blood from pouring down into his mouth, the bedroom door flew open. Ella pushed her way into the room and crouched down beside her mate.

"What the hell?" She turned around and glared at her brother. "What is wrong with you?"

"No, I deserved it." Louis rose to stand back up on his own two feet. "I should've told them earlier."

"Told them what?" Ella's eyes narrowed, and she took a step back.

"That my dad was part of the plan to kill King Corey."

"What?" Ella's brow furrowed, and she shook her head. "But that doesn't make sense. You've got to be lying."

The problem was we could all tell he was speaking the truth. Only, what we didn't know was whether he was holding back any other information.

Watching the scene unfold in front of me caused my heart to drop. Even though it wasn't his fault, this kind of information would've been useful to have from the very start. He was telling the truth now, but why? All the possibilities made my stomach churn.

CHAPTER NINE

"LOOK, I'M SORRY." Louis's nose continued to trickle blood. "I only recently learned about it. I found out about what happened right before we visited with you the first time." He sighed and shook his head. "That's why there was so much tension between the two of us the night of the dinner."

"But why not tell us before now?" Ella's voice was nearing hysteria. "You've been with us for over two months."

"I'm going to kick your ass," Mason growled again. "All this time, and you could have saved half of our efforts? Do you know who the witch is stalking Elena now?"

"Look, I get that you don't trust me." Louis took a step back and drew in a deep breath. "But I overheard Dad on the phone with someone after Darren died. He lost his shit and accidentally told me. We were already disagreeing on a lot of other things, policies, and such."

Louis rubbed his nose. "Shit. This hurts." He shook his head.

"Wait until I get done with you." Mason's body was tense and tight.

"Oh, no you don't." Ella took a menacing step toward her mate. "I'll be the one having the pleasure. I don't care if he's my mate or not. He hurt my family."

"Let's hear him out." If anyone had a right to beat the shit out of him, it was me. Though, royalty wasn't a privilege most of the time. It came with heavy expectations, and sometimes it was void of parental love. "But that doesn't mean we trust him completely. It will take some time to get that trust back."

"That's the problem. You have too big of a heart." Mason's rage was increasing and almost made me dizzy. "I'll be the bad guy."

"No, let's hear him out." The alpha will laced into my words even though I hadn't meant for it to happen.

Mason stiffened and turned to me. "Are you asking as my mate or as the alpha?"

Now, I felt like an asshole. I'd never used the alpha will before and honestly wasn't sure if I even could. "I'm sorry. Of course as your mate. I've never had that happen before."

"She's getting stronger," Tommy said as he stepped into the room with Kassie and Mona.

"Just tell us everything." I reached over and touched Mason's shoulder.

When he stiffened to my touch, I tried not to allow myself to feel hurt.

"It was mainly why we weren't getting along at the dinner party." Louis's nose began to stop bleeding. "He must have decided to try to force your hand into marrying me. But when he realized you had already found your fated, he decided to have me stay and keep tabs on you instead."

"Did you report back to him or something?" Ella's hands trembled with rage.

"He wanted me to, but I didn't." He finally dropped his hands and took a deep breath. "Being around all of you made me feel things I'd never felt before. Being part of a family and then finding my mate. I'm telling you this now because, even though I'd made my choice, I hadn't really said it out loud. This was the last step I had to do in order to leave my lineage behind."

"You think this makes everything okay?" Kassie took a step in his direction.

"He saved my life." I couldn't just turn my back on him no matter how angry I was.

It could've been a convenience thing. Mason's whole body was shaking at this point.

Either way, I couldn't live with myself if I didn't at least give him a chance. Sometimes, people could change. *He never had to tell us if he didn't want to.*

"He's my mate, and I don't buy that shit." Ella's face was tense with pure agony written across it. "You lying, opportunistic piece of shit." Her hands clenched like she was ready to beat the shit out of him. "Did you force the bond on us too?"

"What?" His eyes widened, and he lifted both hands in the air. "God, no. You know I'm not lying. You'd smell it if I was. You're just hurt, and I don't blame you."

"Hey." Mona glanced at Kassie. "Ella, why don't we go into the other room and talk for a second. I think you need a minute before you do something you'll regret."

"What? No." Ella shook her head, making her hair whip from side to side. "I won't regret anything I do to this asshole."

I'm kind of on the same page as her. Mason took another step toward him.

Stop letting your emotions drive this. I was hurt the

same as them, but this might be an opportunity. Maybe we could actually be ahead of the game.

"Why are you telling us this now?" We had to figure out if he was sincere or playing the game. "What changed?"

"I'm afraid my dad might be involved." He took a deep breath and glanced at his shirt coated in blood. "Why else would the alphas be listening to your cousin?"

"When did you come to that conclusion?" Mason's shoulders stayed tensed, but the quivering stopped.

"I'm not sure if he is, but after him busting into the house and how you all accepted me with open arms. It's been weighing on me." Louis took a deep breath without wincing.

His wolf healing was in full force. I wasn't quite sure if I was glad or pissed.

"Why didn't you tell me?" Ella's voice cracked with pain.

"Even though I had nothing to do with King Corey's and Queen Serafina's deaths, I was afraid of how you'd react." Louis licked his lips, wincing when he tasted his blood. "I mean, look at how this is going."

"Don't even try to get sympathy," Ella growled the words. "If you'd just told us from the start ..."

"So, what were you supposed to do while staying with us?" Tommy leaned against the door frame, staring Louis down.

"Nothing really. Just tell him what you all were doing and how your reign was going." Louis glanced at the ground. "Apparently, he and Darren had some kind of agreement, but it didn't pan out. He's wanting to take over the United States wolves as well as his own."

"Why should we believe you're on our side now?" At the end of the day, that's what we needed to know.

"Honestly, I've got nothing." Louis took a deep breath.

"All I can say is," he said as his attention turned to Ella, "that being here with all of you, the love and friendship that you all share together made me realize that I didn't want that kind of throne back home. Each one of you loves each other, and there aren't ulterior motives. Back home, people either wanted to be close to me to get something or for exposure. It's not like that here."

Despite my growing up mainly with Kassie and Mona, I understood where he was coming from. Even at the tender age of six, people had tried manipulating me since I was tied to the crown. My parents tried to protect me, but there was only so much they could do when growing up in the spotlight. Through tragedy, I had gotten a chance to get away from it all and grow up normally. "Well, we got a chance to meet and connect without the throne. That's why I tried to pretend to be human."

"But even if you hadn't, you wouldn't do something like this." Ella turned her head to me with an expression I couldn't read. "Tell him."

"I can't tell you that." I had to be honest even if it made me sound like a bad person. "My parents tried to shield me from the world that Louis described, but there is only so much of it that can be buffered." Even though I wasn't sure if we could trust Louis, I couldn't completely throw him to the wolves either. No pun intended.

"Listen, I had to come clean for you." His eyes turned a dark steel color as they scanned Ella's face. "And for everyone else. I don't know the specifics. Dad refused to tell me, but we had a big enough fight to where I stayed here with you, willing to find distance from him. I had no clue I'd find my mate here. I'm willing to give up everything for you. Hell, I submitted to Elena and saved her when Gabby attacked."

Once again, he was being truthful.

"Just say the word and we can kick him out." Kassie was ready to take him. Her hands were on the handcuffs in her back pocket.

"I think we all need to calm down and take a breath." At the moment, I wasn't sure what the right answer was, but having Louis near us was probably the safest bet. *If we allow him to leave without knowing everything, he could run to his dad and make things even worse.*

Fine, but he sleeps where the guards can keep an eye on him. We can't risk anything happening to my sister. Mason took a step back so he was standing partially in front of me and his sister.

"Ella, I'm sorry. I should've come clean earlier." Louis frowned and avoided her gaze by looking down.

"Look, I love you." She took a deep breath. "But I'm hurt ... I need time."

"Let's eat dinner." Even though the thought now turned my stomach. There was too much at stake to make any hasty decisions. If what he said was the truth, then we might have a little bit of an advantage. King Adelmo would expect us to be knocking down his door or retaliating. I had to keep my head on straight with both Adelmo and Louis. "Then we can go from there."

"Okay." Louis nodded his head and gave me a slight bow. "I appreciate you not kicking me out right away."

"Don't get too comfortable." Mason was so tense he probably couldn't even move if he'd wanted to.

"Why don't you go change shirts?" Between the metallic scented air and all the turmoil that was flooding me from my alpha bond with Mason, I felt like I may puke.

"That's fair." He scanned our group and hurt flowed through all of us. "Okay, I'll go grab a clean shirt."

"I'll go with you." Tommy pointed down the hall to the other side of the suite. "Your bag is in the other guest room. Let's go."

We all watched the two of them as they exited the room and headed down the hall.

Tommy was on full alert while Louis hung his head.

"I ..." Ella took a step back and shook her head. "I don't know what to do with this."

Do you mind if I talk to your sister for a second? I hated to ask Mason to leave right now. Except Ella was about to break down, and she was too strong to want to do it in front of everyone.

Yeah, I think that's a good idea. He turned around and kissed my cheek. *If anything goes wrong, I'll let you know.*

I caught Kassie's and then Mona's eyes, flicking from theirs to the door. Since we couldn't mind speak in human form, it could be inconvenient. Despite that, we had known each other long enough to understand each other even without it.

They nodded in understanding.

"I'm going to go check on the pizza." Mona walked out the door and headed toward the elevator.

"Mason, let's go get the rooms resituated. I'm assuming Ella won't want to share a room with Louis tonight," Kassie huffed. "We'd better figure out the logistics."

"On it." Mason nodded as he walked out the door, following behind Kassie.

Ella moved and shut the door behind them. When the door clicked, I'd expected her to turn back in my direction, but she stayed still.

I could only imagine how much pain she was going through. "Hey, are you okay?" I walked over and placed my hand on her shoulder, forcing her to turn around.

When she did, tears were already running down her face. "I just don't understand."

I pulled her into my arms, wishing I could take all the pain away. "He's in a tough spot."

"You make it sound like you believe him." Her tone was neither warm nor cold; only factual.

"Didn't you notice the tension between him and his father the first night at the NYC apartment?" It was strange even back then, how father and son had reacted to one another. It was almost as if Louis wanted to provoke his dad in every way he could.

"Yeah, but it could all be an act." She pointed toward the door. "And it pisses me off that I still love him." Her words broke off into a sob.

"Of course you do." I ran my hands through her soft, silky hair. "And honestly, I think he's telling the truth."

"But he could be manipulating you." Ella sounded like she wanted me to prove she was wrong.

"He could be." I didn't want to lie and be wrong, but I thought he was being truthful. "But there is no magic in the world strong enough to fake a mate bond. He is yours whether you like it or not."

"So you think there is a chance he really was scared?" Ella wiped the moisture from under her eyes. She stared at me like a child full of hope on Christmas morning.

"I don't think we should write him off yet." I wanted to be reassuring, but I didn't want to be overly optimistic either. "Think about how you'd feel if you learned something so horrid about your father and then get dumped off into another country with three people who weren't accustomed to royal life. You wouldn't want to start singing all your secrets, sharing them with complete strangers. And then, you find your mate, and what if your father's past actions define who they think you are."

"I hadn't thought about it that way." Ella chewed on her bottom lip. "Ugh, I'm so not this girl. I don't pine away for some guy, especially one who's messed up royally."

"Royally, huh?" I needed to make her smile.

"Stop it." She still snorted. "I didn't mean it like that. But you're right. I could see where he would really struggle with it."

"Yes, the truth has a way of coming to light." Even if it took close to thirteen years to do so. "Let's be cautious and see what happens."

"I don't think I can go back to acting normal with him though." Ella took a step back and took a deep breath.

"That's fine. You don't have to." She needed to realize her feelings were just as valid as his. "It might be good for all of us to calm down for the next day or two and see how everything plays out. Making rash decisions in a moment isn't good for anyone."

"You're right." Ella nodded. "I'll sleep wherever Kassie and Mona are tonight. Even though I love him, I need time."

"You do what makes you feel most comfortable with your decisions and your relationship." The last thing I wanted to do was push her into a decision that she might wind up regretting. "There is no right or wrong answer here."

"I'm so glad you're my best friend and my sister." She wrapped her arms around me and hugged me tightly. "I don't know what Mason and I would do without you."

"Well, you'd be leading a normal life, going to parties and underground fights." I winked at her. "You'd probably be studying for some exam right now too, which would probably be better than here."

"Life may be crazy, but I wouldn't have it any other way. And you make my brother happy, so I can't complain about that."

"Food's here!" Mona yelled from down the hall.

"Are you ready to eat?" I needed to be upbeat and light for her.

"Do I breathe oxygen?" Ella arched an eyebrow and grinned despite the sadness still reflecting in her eyes.

"Then let's go." As I opened the bedroom door, I couldn't help but hope I was right. If Louis proved to be on the other side, I wasn't quite sure my best friend would survive, let alone her heart.

CHAPTER TEN

I'D TOSSED and turned all night. Between the bombshell Louis had dropped and my anxiety from not knowing what to expect at tomorrow's breakfast, sleep was impossible.

I squirmed away from Mason's body and rolled so I could glance at the clock. It said five in the morning.

Great. I wanted to get up but didn't want to wake him or the girls.

After the awkward dinner, the girls decided to take the pull out sofa and couch to guard the elevator while Louis took the other large king room. Tommy had insisted on sleeping on the floor of Louis's room to ensure he didn't sneak out or something..

We actually had a whole pizza left over which was a testament to how upset Ella truly was. She only managed to eat half a pizza instead of her usual full one.

What are you doing? Mason's voice was thick with sleep even in my head. He scooted over to me and pulled me back into his arms. *It's way too early for your brain to begin running.*

I could only wish it had just started now. I was

exhausted but couldn't do a damn thing about it. *It's been a long night.*

His lips found my neck, and he lightly kissed it. *Why didn't you wake me?*

There was no reason for neither one of us to get some sleep. I closed my eyes, enjoying the feel of him.

Everything is going to be all right. He took a deep breath, and his hands slipped under my nightshirt. *Especially after I kill Louis.*

You will not. I wanted to chastise him, but his hands were beginning to do things that made my brain sizzle. *What are you doing? You need your rest.*

I'm thinking of something I might need more. His hands caressed my breasts, making my body begin to burn and ache.

I turned over so I was facing him, slamming my lips against his and enjoying the feel of his fingers digging into my back. I took a deep breath and ran my fingers across his muscles. I loved the fact that he slept shirtless.

He tugged at my shorts, removing them from my body. *You always feel so good and soft.*

That better not be a fat joke. I pulled away, still trying to tug his pants down.

Of course it isn't. He chuckled as he grabbed my hand. *Here, let me help you with that.* He finished removing his pajama bottoms and rolled on top of me. *Maybe we can work off some of your excess energy.*

I'm obviously okay with that plan. He slid in between my legs as he kissed down my neck. When he reached my breast, he kissed and gently bit, causing me to moan.

Then, he slammed into me, hitting the right spot inside. I raised up while kissing him and dug my nails into his back.

His smell surrounded me, and his feelings crashed into mine.

Needing to be in control, I pushed him off me and rolled over on top. *You said I needed to exert my excess energy. You shouldn't do all the work.* I guided him inside me, closing my eyes, relishing his feelings and the way our bodies moved in sync. As I rode him, he raised his hips, paying attention to every part of me, and soon we were both releasing, riding the waves of ecstasy.

My body sagged against his, and he stared at me with his eyes full of love.

He grabbed my waist and laid me down beside him. *I don't think I'll ever get tired of doing that.*

You better not. I cuddled into his chest as his fingers ran along my back. *Every time is better than the last.*

That's a good thing since we need to start having all those kids soon. He lowered his mouth to mine and ran his fingers through my hair. *It'll take a lot of practice to make sure it takes. I'm thinking at least three or four times a day.*

That sounds like heaven. The thought of leaving this place behind and only focusing on him filled my head with naughty thoughts. *When things calm down, we may just need to get on it.*

Really? His voice was filled with hope.

I had only been kidding, but the thought made me happy. *Actually, I really do.*

Why wait until then? His hands traveled downward until there was a knock at the door.

Of course, we'd be interrupted now. His upset tone filled my head.

At least, we got the first round out of the way. I kissed his lips again in frustration. My body had already begun responding to his touch once more.

"Elena?" Ella's voice filled the air. "Are you awake?"

"She is now," Mason grumbled.

"Give us a second." I didn't want her walking in while we were both naked.

Why? If she comes in and finds us this way, she'll leave in a hurry. I can't leave you all flustered. His hand continued downward and touched my most sensitive places. His mouth covered mine, swallowing my moan and increasing the pace of his fingers. It wasn't long before I began orgasming again, taking me completely by surprise.

"Are you really going to leave me here like that after the shit night?" Ella's voice sounded hurt.

"No, we're getting dressed." Mason grinned like the devil as he climbed out of the bed to slip his clothes back on.

My body was heavy, so it was my love for her that got me to my feet and throwing my own clothes back on. "Come on in."

The door opened immediately, and she entered the room. She looked directly at me and frowned. "I couldn't sleep all night."

Now, that was something I could sympathize with. "Me neither." I sat on the bed and patted the spot in front of me for her to sit down.

"I'm surprised you're up so early." She arched an eyebrow at Mason. "Normally, waking you up is like pulling teeth."

"Eh, Elena was upset, and I had to take one for the team." He winked at me as he said the words.

"Ew ..." Ella wrinkled her nose and shook her head. "I so did not need to know that. The smell is bad enough. Ugh!"

"You brought it up," Mason grumbled as he padded off to the bathroom.

I glanced at the time again and realized it was after

seven. Time had flown by. "I do need to get in the shower and get ready for the meeting. Are you and Louis going to join us?"

"Yeah, I think so." She ran her hands through her hair. "I'm going to go talk to him now. I think you're right. We need to give him a shot. It just hurt so bad to know what he'd been hiding from me."

"That's probably a good idea." I patted her shoulder and then pulled her in for a hug. "Go talk to him, and then get ready. We all need to be in a decent headspace before going downstairs. This meeting is too important to blow."

"You're right." She hugged me back and headed toward the door. "Wish me luck."

The seven of us loaded into the elevator, heading down to the ground floor to the hotel restaurant.

"If anything looks out of order, we have to leave immediately." Kassie turned toward me and stared into my eyes. "This isn't negotiable, not this time. We have no idea what he may be up to."

"No, I get it." I took a step toward Mason, and he wrapped an arm around my waist, causing my blue button-down shirt to raise up slightly above my black slacks.

Louis stood tense and silent in the back section of the elevator. Ella was next to him, and they were holding hands.

At least, there was that.

The door opened on the bottom floor, and Tommy stepped off first, scanning the area. "Let's go."

"I'll take the rear," Mona called from the back.

"Have you ever met Brent before?" I glanced at Kassie. I figured she had, but we'd never really discussed it before.

"Yes, but it was before your parents died." Kassie still struggled with my parents' death too. "He was new to the role and overly ambitious. Your father had been concerned."

Great, so this might have been an ongoing problem that had no bearing on my father's death.

So, there is no telling how he might have been influenced for the past thirteen years. Mason grumbled the words in our link.

We can speculate all day, but we won't know until we get there. That's what had kept me awake all night. All that stress wasn't helping anyone. *We've got each other, so that's all that matters.*

We entered a large open room with circular tables strategically placed throughout. The hostess walked over to us and smiled. "Hi, how many do you have today?"

"Eight, but someone may already be here waiting on us." We were right on time.

"No, not that we're aware of." She smiled and waved her hand to the room. "Let's go get you seated."

"We'd like something toward the back wall." Kassie pointed to an open table that was set up so we could look straight back and see the kitchen to the far left with a booth butted against the wall and four chairs on the other side.

"Oh ..." The hostess seemed taken off guard. "Sure. We can do that." She waved us to follow behind her, so Tommy went first with Kassie and Mona was bringing up the rear.

When we arrived at the table, the hostess placed the menus at each spot and glanced at me. "If you give me your name, I'll make sure to point your party in the right direction."

"Of course, it's Elena ..." I almost said Hawthrone, but officially, that wasn't my name any longer. Not since Mason and I had gotten married and performed the official mating ceremony. "Lockly."

It's funny. That's the first time you've had to say your name since we got married. I love the way it sounds. Mason took my hand in his and winked at me.

Yeah, I need to get used to it. I liked the way it sounded too.

"I'm going to sit here and keep an eye out from the kitchen." Kassie sat in the last seat, facing the wall."

"I'll sit across from you." Tommy nodded his head. "Mona, can you sit on the other end of the booth? That way we can both scan the room, specifically the high traffic areas."

"Got it." Mona motioned for both Mason and me to slide through. "You two need to be between Tommy and me."

Not wanting to argue and with the tension so high, I obeyed. I slid across the seat so I was positioned between Mason and Mona.

"Well, all right then." Louis sat right across from Mason. "I want to buffer Ella."

He didn't need to say anything else. None of us knew what to expect, and obviously, they had an ally who used magic. I felt his concern, and this relieved me a little as he was thinking of protecting his mate.

Ella sat, her face was tense, and her usual spark was gone.

This all had to end and soon.

"Do you think he'll actually show?" Ella picked up the menu, scanning it.

"Yeah, he'll show." Louis frowned and shook his head. "He wouldn't get any additional backing for removing Elena and Mason if he didn't at least appear to be playing his part."

"Why would that matter?" Ella's forehead creased and brows furrowed.

"Because then it looks like I tried reaching out to him and he refused." I hated politics, yet here I sat waiting. "That could paint at least some level of doubt in people's minds if they find out. So he has to make sure the picture is clear that we're the bad guys."

"However, that doesn't mean he won't show up late." Louis shook his head as he grabbed a menu too.

"I wish people would just say what they mean." Mason's voice was deep with anger. "There's no need for all these games."

"Oh, but there is." Louis glanced at Ella out of the corner of his eye. "You see, the games have been around for years. If you aren't careful, then you are viewed as weak. There is a reason why secrets are kept and also for when secrets are revealed."

"What are you getting at?" I asked. He was hinting at something. "Stop being coy."

"No." He lifted his hands in the air. "I don't know anything. I'm just saying we need to be more careful. My father and I are on opposite sides of the fence now, and he's a little bit unpredictable. We can't remove him from the equation."

Do you believe him? Mason stared Louis down.

Yeah, I do. I cleared my throat and picked up a glass of water that had already been poured before we sat down and took a sip. My nerves were on edge, and I needed to feel in control of something.

"What do you think your father is up to?" Ella turned her body so she faced Louis and stared into his eyes.

"I'm not sure."

"See ..." Ella pointed at him.

"Let me finish, please." Louis sighed and cleared his throat. "If I was a betting man, I think my father would be working with Richard. You see, Richard needs help, and if my father helps him, then he can leverage something in return that would benefit him greatly."

"What do you think it is?" We had the one person who probably knew King Adelmo the best sitting right in front of us. Now that he had told us his little secret, he should be more forthcoming.

"Power. Control in some way." Louis ran his hand down his face. "He'd have to get something out of it. To be honest, I'm still not sure what Darren had promised him, but it never came through."

"The only way I could think of him getting more power is by owning territories in the United States." That's when everything became at least somewhat clear. "He wants to control the U.S. That's why he tried to pretend my dad and he had an agreement with our engagement."

"Dad had always said that you guys didn't know what you were doing over here. That if you took control and used the resources wisely, you could control the world from your own castle overseas." Louis shook his head and frowned. "Effectively making another regime solely reliable for the welfare of your people."

"There are so many ways that could happen." Mason shook his head and furrowed his eyebrows. "I mean, it could be physically over them; as in having some kind of voting structure in place where he'd have weight in any decision made here."

"Holy shit." Tommy's voice was deep and sounded shocked while Mona jumped to her feet.

They never acted that way unless something was really

wrong. My eyes followed to where he was staring and locked with blue eyes almost the same shade as my own.

Richard was standing next to the Atlanta alpha and looking my way with a huge smirk on his face.

We were stuck and not able to do anything about it because of all the humans in the room. This was some kind of power play, and they certainly had the upper hand.

CHAPTER ELEVEN

"THAT'S IT. WE'RE LEAVING." Mason's voice was deep with a hint of violence.

"We can't." I wanted to walk out that door as badly as he did. Only then, they'd know they got to us, and we couldn't show weakness. "We can't act any differently. Otherwise, we react in the exact way they want us to."

"They want us to make a scene." Louis didn't turn around and kept his eyes trained on us. "Anything out of sorts will make them happy. They'll know they have leverage and control over you."

"How about I bitch slap them and put them in their place." Ella started turning, but Louis touched her shoulder.

"Seriously, don't react." Louis touched her arm, bringing her attention to him.

He's right. Even though I didn't grow up as a royal, my first six years were enough to at least give me a glimpse into this world. I wasn't completely cold, not the way that was expected of heirs from a young age. *Don't react, and we can't make a scene with the humans. That'll only prove we're unfit to rule.*

When this is all over, I'm going to kick their asses. Mason took a deep breath and forced his shoulders to relax.

You and me both. He wasn't going to get to have all the fun.

The two assholes made their way over to our table with the hostess in tow.

"Is it okay if we just add a chair at the end of the table since they're already seated?" There was a nervous twinge in her voice as if she knew this was a very uncomfortable situation.

"That's perfectly fine." Richard's deep, creepy voice answered her.

"Great." She took a seat from the vacant table next to us and put it on the end between Mona and Brent.

"Thank you, gorgeous." Richard cooed as he plopped into the seat. "Please, go ahead and sit next to the European Prince."

"As long as you're sure." Brent pulled out the chair and got comfortable. "Hello, Elena."

He didn't say queen and did it on purpose. He was going to do everything he could to let me know that he didn't recognize me as his leader.

"Hello, Brent." My tone was level and clear despite the fact that I wanted to come unglued. This guy had an overvalued sense of self-worth. "It's been a while since we've seen each other."

"Yes, I believe we met a few weeks prior to your parents' deaths." He said the words so flippantly as if it wasn't life-changing. "You still look like the same little girl who didn't understand the world, and of course, your actions have proven it."

He wanted to play ball, but what he didn't realize was that I didn't have to do it with him. "If by not understanding the world, you mean coming here immediately to kiss your ass, you're right. That's not how my world works."

"And you're classless as well." He turned his focus on Mason. "And for a king, you claimed someone who was born common and didn't have the balls to take over his father's pack when he came of age."

"I don't have a problem throwing the challenge down to you." Mason's jaw clenched, and he took in a deep ragged breath.

He wants you to react that way. I needed Mason to rein it in. *Calm down, or we'll prove whatever Richard has told him.*

"Aw, and the subpar upbringing comes to light." Brent arched his eyebrows, causing them to disappear under his sandy blond hair, and he pulled at the edges of his goatee. "You were right about that."

"I would disagree with that." Louis turned his head in Brent's direction and grinned. "At least, with them, you know exactly where they stand."

"For a prince, I'd expect better from you." Brent tsked as he shook his head.

"It's not about letting people know where they stand but having the strength to do what's right." Richard's arrogant voice floated across the table.

At this very moment, I wanted to take my dull knife and slice his neck.

"Hi, can I take your order?" An older lady smiled awkwardly as she took in our table. "Or should I come back later?" She took a step back as if she was trying to gain distance from us.

Great, we're making a scene. I took a deep breath and smiled. "I'd love a coffee and some eggs and bacon."

The others followed suit, and soon the lady was walking away.

"So, you wanted me here." Brent leaned back in his seat and spread his arms apart. "I'm here. What is it that you want to discuss?"

"Forgive me if I'm not willing to be so forthcoming when there is someone present that was involved in my parents' murder." I wasn't going to name the elephant in the room. Even though there was no reason to pretend that he wasn't here.

"See, I told you that's what she'd say." Richard rolled his eyes and crossed his arms. "She had the audacity to kill my father and tries to pretend it was us that are the bad guys."

"That's bullshit, and you know it." Mona's normally sweet disposition was gone. "You're no better than your father."

"I tend to agree with Richard." Brent's brown eyes darkened. "I mean it seems largely convenient that you somehow remained alive and then killed his father. I think there's way more to the story than you're sharing."

"It's a shame that you're just an evil, opportunistic prick like good ol' Dick here." Ella's hazel eyes narrowed as she leaned over her mate. "What'd they promise you?"

"You should never talk to an alpha that way." Brent shook his head and wrinkled his nose in disgust.

"Then, earn the respect." Mason leaned closer to me, wrapping his arm around my shoulder. "You came in here with him, of all people, and you're wondering why this isn't going well."

"I don't need this to go well." Brent stared Mason in the eyes. "You are the ones trying to mend the rift that you created. I'm assuming the Chicago alphas warned you about what we're planning."

"We've been in power for only a handful of months and had wars we had to battle. Did you expect us to drop everything to make our rounds throughout the entire country?" It pissed me off that he was acting so cavalier. It's not like we were locking ourselves in our house, refusing to come out as my uncle had done.

"You visited Chicago." He arched an eyebrow. "But didn't even bother attempting to come here."

"Because the vampires took a pack member and were torturing him." Mason's voice lowered and turned into a growl.

"One pack member's safety isn't as important as the millions of other wolves who need a queen and king who take care of them." Brent shook his head. "That's what a true king and queen know."

"I told you that you weren't important to them." Richard shook his head and closed his eyes. "Even though Dad didn't visit, he made sure your city got the financing it needed to become a bigger paranormal city and the protection that it needed. He was so scared and heartbroken to leave after what had happened to Corey, but he always called you regularly to check on you."

So this is what had happened. Darren financed the city, growing it bigger so they could charge the supernaturals more for traveling back and forth. It wasn't to help our people; it was to take advantage of them.

"When did he actually help your pack?" I couldn't believe how easily he was being manipulated. "My parents were killed, and I'm still sitting before you today."

"Being young is thinking you're indestructible. Believe me, I know." He shifted in his seat. "But King Darren gave us funding to keep the hub brimming. We've got new hotel rooms, restaurants, everything we need to cater to the supernatural needs."

"That's not taking care of your people." Mason chuckled hard. "When someone was sick, did they offer aid? When something went wrong, did they offer protection?"

"That's what I'm here for." Brent frowned, and his eyes began to glow.

Holy shit. This guy had an ego.

Cups clanged together, causing all of our attention to turn to the poor waitress who obviously felt uncomfortable waiting on us. Her face was pale, which was saying something for her. "Here are your drinks." She passed them out quickly as Mason and Brent glared at each other, only adding to her anxiety.

This was going well.

She scurried off, leaving even more tension in the air somehow.

"You're right, tending to your pack is your job." No wonder this guy gets along with Richard. He had to be more about making money and maintaining status than his pack's wellbeing, which meant there was no way I could right this wrong. We'd insulted him by not visiting, and no excuse would resonate with him. "But it's ours too. The other packs needed our help. Vampires were attacking our kind. As far as we know, that hasn't been happening here."

"Of course not." He cleared his throat and glanced at his glass.

He was lying. His heart began beating faster, and the smell of rotten eggs surrounded us.

"Is that so?" Mason narrowed his eyes as if he was going in for the kill.

Don't do it. The last thing we needed to do was bruise

his ego more. *It'll only make things worse, and he already knows we know. Let it slide.*

I glanced at Ella, worried she would go off too, but she and Louis were looking each other in the eye. He was handling her for me. Thank God for that.

"Are you doubting me?" Brent lifted his chin in the air, trying to regain some semblance of control.

"It's good news." I locked eyes with him and arched an eyebrow. I was going to make him break eye contact with me. "So no other random things are happening that would warrant us providing your people with some help?"

"He already said no." Richard's voice raised, and the words were rushed. "Do you want to keep insulting him?"

"Oh, dear cousin." I wanted to barf at the words, but I forced them out without wincing somehow. "I'm not insulting him. We only want to make sure that we don't need to offer more protection or help with any endeavors involving any of the other supernatural races."

Something almost akin to doubt filled his eyes. "No, everything is fine here." He cleared his throat and grabbed the cup of coffee that had been placed in front of him. "Why were the other places being attacked?"

"Not sure." That wasn't a lie. They'd said that they'd been having issues with the vampires before my arrival. "They just stated that the vampires had gotten out of control and were acting a little more brazen than in the past."

"That has to be an overstatement." Richard placed his hands on the table.

He chose his words carefully. My stomach soured at how well my family was at manipulating everything.

This whole thing is ridiculous. Mason was becoming more and more agitated. "Well, seeing as you weren't there, how would you know?"

"Because he's a know-it-all that lies through his teeth." Ella stared him down.

"I don't have to stay here and be insulted." Richard pushed back and stood. "I thought we could come here and talk family to family, but all you're doing is throwing accusations at me and my parents."

"It'd probably be best if we left." Brent stood as well and glanced at me. "I'm sorry, but I'll be petitioning for your cousin to take the crown. You falsely accused his father of attempted murder and locked your own family up in prison. You hadn't even bothered to call or check on the southern packs until you heard of our move against your reign. It proves that you have favoritism and are only out for your best interests." He cleared his throat and nodded at Richard. "Let's go."

Despite his entire speech, there was something about his eyes. Uncertainty or maybe even fear shone there.

"And I expected better of you, young prince." Richard scowled at Louis and shook his head. "This won't bode well for you."

The two of them turned, heading toward the door, leaving us all in the aftermath.

"What the fuck was that?" Ella's voice was a little too loud, making the closest table to us turn in our direction.

"Calm down," Mona warned.

"Hey, at least, I waited this long." Ella pointed her finger at Louis. "You better be glad I love you or you'd be missing an important appendage, considering how many times you told me to stay quiet."

"I'm not scared." He picked up a glass of water and took a sip. "You would never cut that off. It would be just as much of a punishment for you as me."

"Please, for the love of God, don't say that in front of

me." Mason closed his eyes and shook his head. "There are some things I don't want to know about."

"Like what I had to hear this morning when I knocked on your door?" Ella tilted her head to the side.

"You knocked on our bedroom door. You were asking for it." He pointed at the table. "You're doing that here at a table where we're all in front of people."

"Can we focus on what's important here?" I loved these two, but what had gone down was not good. "We have a serious threat."

"They couldn't possibly get enough votes, could they?" Louis leaned back when he took in my face.

"What votes?" Mason glanced between the two of us.

"If more than half of the United States alphas vote against you two as King and Queen, Richard could be appointed to the position." Kassie shook her head, and her face was a shade red with pure anger. "I never thought someone would stoop so low."

"Is that even possible?" Mason pulled me closer to his side. "I mean I'd never heard about it."

"It is but extremely rare." Tommy shook his head as the waitress appeared in front of us again.

"Here is your food." She began passing the plates out but paused when she got to Richard and Brent's vacant seats. "Uh, are they coming back?"

"No, but go ahead and set it down." Ella pointed at the open spot in front of her. "I stress eat."

The lady began to giggle and stopped when Ella didn't laugh with her. "Oh, you're being serious."

"Hell yeah, I am."

"Okay, here you go." She placed the plates on the table and ran off.

Ella grabbed her fork, stabbed three pieces of sausage, and crammed them into her mouth. "Te' me m'r."

A laugh escaped me. I needed that. "If he gets more than half of the alphas to side with him, we could be overthrown."

"That just means that the attacks are going to ramp up." Louis shook his head, and his shoulders tensed. "They're going to make sure we're preoccupied."

I hadn't even considered that possibility, but he could be right. If we were busy with our own, personal attacks or attacks on other packs, we wouldn't be able to visit the rest of the packs to gain support on our side. I wasn't sure how the hell to proceed from here.

CHAPTER TWELVE

I SHOVED my clothes back into the duffle bag that Mason and I shared.

"What did that bag ever do to you?" Mason strolled from the bathroom to our bedroom. He had a small smile spread across his face, but his eyes were tight, and his muscles tensed.

Our entire group had been a bundle of nerves since we left breakfast. "Its compliance is threatening. It's not being difficult like every other alpha out there."

"Yeah, but don't worry. I'm sure it'll get ornery on the plane ride and pop open or something." He walked over and placed his hands on my shoulders.

"Do you think we should go to Nashville first before heading home?" That was the other alpha who was giving us apprehension, and he was tight with Brent. It seemed hopeless.

"Maybe." He took a deep breath. "I didn't expect this to be so hard."

"You thought being a ruler wouldn't be difficult?" I

couldn't blame him. No one really knew what royal life was like. It wasn't one that was easy to explain.

"Well, yeah." He wrapped his arms around my waist and pulled me close. "Every pack has an alpha that takes care of them. I figured the top alpha didn't have to worry about much. Boy, was I wrong."

"A lot of people don't see behind the scenes." I took a deep breath and couldn't believe that it was already turning dark outside. We'd come back up to the room right after the meeting, and each one of us began to fall apart in a way. No one could decide on what the correct next step would be, but we all agreed it wasn't staying here. Brent may have doubts now, but he wasn't going to risk turning on Richard. It would take a miracle for that to happen.

"It's really easy for packs to misunderstand how busy royals truly are." He sighed. "I hate that I was so blind."

"It's not your fault. My dad always said in order to be an effective ruler, others shouldn't know you're struggling." Those words were uttered to me one night after my mother's last relative had died. It was her father, and he had always been instrumental to hers and my life. We had to meet with several alphas the night of the funeral, and I broke down crying in my room. He'd pulled me aside and spoke those words to me. "You should always hold your head high even when you're sad. As long as you appear strong, others will never underestimate you. It's not fair, but being picked for this life is not a choice. It's a destiny. He then wrapped his arms around me, told me he loved me and to cry it out before we went downstairs. We were twenty minutes late because both he and I mourned my grandfather together."

"Wow, your dad was a great man." He spun me around

and stared into my eyes. "He'd be so proud of you. Hell, I'm sure he is as he watches from above."

"I hope so. Can you believe he got accused of being insensitive with their time and that a true king would not make their people wait?" I remembered being so pissed. Though instead of explaining why or being rude, he only nodded his head and told them he understood. That something had come up and that it wouldn't happen again.

A knock on our open door had us turning toward it. Kassie was there, and her face was a shade more pale than usual.

"What's wrong?" Whatever it was, it wouldn't be good.

"We just got a call from Brent." Instead of being angry though, she looked scared.

I growled. "What's going on?" Did they already have enough votes to eradicate Mason and me from the crown? I knew Brent had pull with several alphas, but I didn't think it could happen that quickly.

"No, they're being attacked ... slaughtered really." Kassie took a deep breath. "He's asked for help."

"You expect us to want to walk in and help him after everything he just did?" Mason's body was stiff.

"Of course we are. They are our people." It's strange that right after our meeting, something like that would happen. "It's not their fault he's an opportunistic ass."

"You're right. Dammit." Mason frowned.

"That's what I figured you'd say. You always gotta go running off into danger." Kassie huffed, but there was relief in her eyes. She cared about our people as much as we did. "Tommy is already pulling the car around. Mona, Ella, and Louis are already at the elevator."

"We'll stay another night after all." I picked up the duffle bag and ran out the door. Might as well stay. They were going to charge us for the night anyway.

Kassie and Mason walked quickly behind me and caught up when I met with the rest of our group.

"I'll protect everyone except for Brent." Ella narrowed her eyes as she wrinkled her nose like she'd smelled something disgusting. "That asshole deserves to get hurt."

The elevator dinged, and the six of us entered it.

"I'm with Ella on this one." Mason chuckled.

"You both don't mean it." They were full of shit. They may not like him, but they would never let one of our own get injured. If he was calling us, that must mean he was singing a different tune.

"Let us have our moment," Ella grumbled as Louis shook his head with a small grin.

The door opened up when we got to the bottom floor, and Kassie hurried off to check the lobby. "Come on." She waved us on, letting us know the room was clear of visible threats.

"I know I haven't earned your trust yet, but do you think this could be a setup?" Louis followed closely behind us, and his tone was a little on edge. "This could be a trap."

"He's right." Mason stopped in his tracks.

"It's not." Mona frowned. "We had someone we trust run by and check it out before we alerted Elena and Mason."

"Wait." That wasn't necessarily a good thing. "How long has this attack been going on?"

"Only about thirty minutes." Mona waved her hands as she pointed to our Suburban pulled in front. "Now let's go. It'll take about that same amount of time to get there."

We all climbed into the vehicle, and Tommy took off as soon as the back door shut.

We turned off the main road onto a small gravel driveway. The vehicle bounced, jostling us from side to side.

"Where the hell are we going?" Ella cried in the backseat. "These two," she said as she pointed to Louis on one side and Mona on the other, "are not graceful and keep falling all over me. The next thing I know, we're going to hear a banjo."

"It's not a movie." Mason chuckled as he grabbed his armrests, preventing him from being jostled as bad as her.

The trees broke apart ahead of us and soon it opened up to a large subdivision. It reminded me of James's pack, but the houses were bigger, and there were more of them.

The yards had to be close to an acre apart, and there were vampires everywhere. It was a huge fight, and there were even a few dead bodies that littered the ground.

"Oh, dear God." I unlocked my door and jumped out. "It's a massacre."

As I began to run toward an older shifter who had a vampire on top of her, a hand grabbed my wrist, jerking me backward.

I can't lose you. Please, please stay near me. Mason's eyes pleaded with me.

I had to do something or he'd be too distracted and get hurt himself. *Fine, but we've got to hurry.*

Not wanting to waste any additional time, I shifted to my wolf. When I got close, I saw that the vampire had his hands around her neck, getting ready to strangle her. I growled and jumped on top of him, clamping my teeth around his throat, and ripped away, tearing it out.

Something hissed, and I turned around to face another vampire who had its sights set on me. He was about to attack when Mason appeared in his wolf form and steamrolled the guy at least ten feet away from me.

While Mason took care of him, I scanned the area, looking for anything that stood out to me.

A sandy-haired wolf ran in my direction and stared into my eyes.

It had to be Brent. He whined and nodded in the direction of a house that was three houses over.

If he thought I would blindly follow him, he was stupid. It could be a set up even though I doubted Brent would allow his pack to be killed off like this. *I think this is Brent. He wants me to follow him.* I linked both with my guards and Mason.

Whoa. Did you just give us a heads up about you doing something that could be dangerous? Kassie sounded impressed.

Don't make a big deal out of it or she won't keep doing it. Mona chastised as if she wasn't in a huge fight right now. She jumped on the back of a vampire who was fighting another shifter and clamped on to his arm, dragging him off.

The shifter was then able to get off the ground and start fighting again.

Come on. Mason ran up next to me, and we followed after Brent, running to the house he had indicated.

When we came within fifty feet, I heard low moaning and whimpering.

It sounded as if someone was in incredible pain. I rushed over and found a pregnant shifter lying on the ground, clutching her unborn child within her abdomen.

Someone is hurt. I called out to the bond.

There are a lot of people hurt right now, Elena. Ella's tone was full of annoyance. *Being a little more specific might bode well for us all.*

Stop being a smartass right now. Mason jogged over to the woman and sniffed her. *She's got internal bleeding.*

We need to help her. If we didn't help her, both she and the baby could die.

If we don't take care of the vampires, then no one here is going to last long. Kassie's voice was raspy and low.

She was right. It's not like we could take care of her now. *Go, I'll stay here and protect her.*

I don't want to leave you. Mason was torn.

The sooner we kill the vampires, the quicker we can leave and get help for this mother.

No one is over here now. I walked over to the woman and smelled her again. She had Brent's musky scent on her.

He trotted over again, and before it hit me, he bowed his head. *I'm sorry I doubted you, My Queen. Please, we've got to help my mate.*

Right now, we need to get rid of the vampires and get your healer. I stared into his eyes and took a step forward. *Go help the others, and I'll stay with her.*

He nodded his head. Soon, both he and Mason were heading to help the others. I sat next to her, keeping my eyes open and listening for anything that sounded out of place.

All I could do was listen to her faint breathing and the sounds of fighting less than fifty yards away. I took a deep breath and closed my eyes, but when I opened them, there was a huge, muscular vampire right in front of me.

"I've been waiting for you to show up." He shook with laughter. He had a scar that started right above his eyebrow and ended at the top of his upper lip.

I stood on all four legs and growled.

"Don't worry." The vampire waggled his eyebrows at me, and his black eyes flashed as a menacing grin slowly filled his face. "It's you that I'm interested in." He flashed, and before I could process it, he lifted me over his head. "This might hurt a little." He chuckled at his own joke as he threw me down hard.

My body crashed into the ground, and I heard a popping sound come from my leg. I landed on my right side and felt like I was crushed; the pain was excruciating.

"I thought you'd put up more of a fight than that." The vampire began heading slowly in my direction again, enjoying the predatory side of himself.

Using every ounce of energy in my body, I stood on all fours and turned to stare him down. *I need help.* I had a feeling I wasn't going to make it out of this one alive. I refused to let him see how hurt I was though. Showing weakness would make it more fun for him.

On my way. Mason's voice was determined, and he appeared behind the vampire in seconds. His now auburn coat glowing in the dusk.

I hadn't really seen him as a wolf since he became king, and to see his usual black coat now auburn startled me. He must have been on his way when I got hurt since I wasn't blocking the mate bond. He probably sensed I was in pain.

I needed to act as though I was in more pain than I actually was so the vampire would focus on me. I let my weakness show by holding my broken hind leg in the air. That sick, sadistic bastard's grin grew even wider. He was so immersed in the hunt that he didn't notice the wolf that was readying to strike at him from behind.

Mason ran right at him, lowering himself to the ground and knocking the vampire's feet out from under him. The vampire hit the ground hard, landing on his back.

"What the ..." The words were a hiss as the guy glanced behind him and locked eyes with my mate.

A loud growl was Mason's response.

The vampire jumped to his feet and narrowed his eyes. "This makes my job easier with you both being here." He flashed and reached for Mason's neck.

Just as he was about to close his hand, Mason jerked back and clamped down on his hand.

"Shit." The vampire tried slinging Mason off, but all it did was make Mason clamp down even harder.

I had to do something now. I took a deep breath, determined to work through the pain. I took off running and almost stumbled at first, but soon began to limp, making it somewhat bearable. There was no way in hell I was going to be able to jump, so I did the only thing I knew to do. I bit into his leg.

"Agh, you bitch!" The vampire glanced behind him and began kicking the leg my teeth were sunk into.

I wanted to whimper because he was forcing some weight on my injury. However, I held it back. No matter what he did, I had to keep a firm hold.

He reached down with his free hand and grabbed my throat, cutting off my airway.

Mason let go of his hand and jumped for his neck.

The vampire once again threw me to the ground and caught Mason before he could latch on.

I didn't land quite as hard this time, but between the already injured leg and my low oxygen, the world began to spin. I took deep breaths, needing to stay conscious and help.

The vampire had Mason by the face and brought his bloodied hand up, aiming his fingers at Mason's eyes.

Oh, hell no. I struggled up on all fours, relieved that my broken foot was beginning to heal. I rushed the vampire and was able to leverage some strength to jump and bite into his shoulder.

He groaned in pain and reared back, throwing Mason ten feet away, slamming him into a tree.

A large yelp sounded as his body bounced off the tree and landed on the ground.

Mason. I yelled in our bond as I let go of the vampire and hit the ground, desperate to get to him. Right when I thought I might be able to pass the vampire, he yanked me back.

"Where do you think you're going?" The vampire jerked me by the back of my neck and turned me so I was looking into his face. He pulled me closer and took a huge sniff. "And people said you'd be hard to beat." His dark laughter rang in my ears.

I had to end this and now. I steadied myself and swung my front legs forward. As my claws touched his neck, I sunk them into his skin.

"Agh!" He tore me away, causing my neck to snap away from him, and then tossed me onto the ground.

Luckily, I was able to control the speed and land on all fours without further injury. I had to get to Mason and check on him. *Are you okay?* I wanted to look at him, but the vampire would attack.

I'm fine. His voice was faint but there.

Now that I knew he was okay; I could focus on the vampire. The asshole had to go down. *I'm going in.*

Distract him so his back turns to me. Mason's voice was strengthening. *Do whatever you need to, and I'll surprise him from the back.*

Okay, I could do that. I took a deep breath and pretended to charge the vampire. When he appeared ready for my attack, I swung around him and turned back around so I could face him.

When he turned his back to Mason, I was tempted to break out into a little dance.

"Getting scared?" The vampire laughed as if he had told a great joke. "I told her I'd get you." He charged at me, blending together with his speed. I took a quick breath and then rolled out of the way. He ran past me and almost reached the broken pregnant girl in the front yard.

Not wanting him to turn around and see Mason getting closer to me, I rushed and jumped onto his back, thrashing the skin on his neck.

"Agh!" He groaned as he tried to reach over his shoulders to grab me. He managed to get a hold of my uninjured foot and began yanking, but it was enough of a distraction for Mason to launch.

My mate's auburn fur coat jumped past me, and his teeth sunk into the front of the bewildered vampire. Before he could do anything else, Mason ripped out his throat.

As the vampire fell to the ground, I unlatched and fell down on all fours.

There was a huge thud as the vampire hit, and soon his body began to disintegrate.

Mason rushed over to me and checked me all over. *Are you okay?*

I'm fine. I glanced at his side and saw blood pooling there. *You need to sit down.*

No, I'm fine. He licked my face. *It's already healing. We need to go check on the others.*

My heart sunk. I could feel the pack's link to me and could tell there were several hurt and injured. A few seemed wounded enough to dim from my bond. *Yes, we have to hurry.*

CHAPTER THIRTEEN

BRENT RUSHED INTO THE CLEARING, looked at Mason and me, and then his mate. *Is she okay? Were you attacked?*

Yes, we were, and she's about the same. I needed to get back to my people.

Stay with her. Mason commanded him as he turned to run back in the direction of the fight where everyone else was still trying to gain the upper hand.

We'll be back soon, I promised. But I couldn't stay back any longer. Mason was as desperate as I was to get back to help everyone else. He was feeling the struggles too.

Fine. I'll let you know if we need help. Brent's tone wasn't condescending but tired.

As we rushed back into the clearing, I wasn't expecting what I saw. Kassie was taking out what had to be the last of the vampires. Ash blew in the air, and there were several injured wolves along with a few dead on the ground.

My heart broke. We needed to bury them.

Oh my God, you scared me. Ella ran over to me in her wolf form. Her blonde fur matched her hair. *Are you okay?*

There were a few bite marks on her but nothing really worrisome. Most of them had already healed. *Yeah, there was a vampire waiting for me. That's all.* I was already healed, but Mason was still limping.

Where's everyone else? Mason glanced around, looking for our guards and Louis.

Louis's light auburn wolf came trotting to us. He had deep gouges on his sides and his breathing was ragged. *The guards are coming back around.* He jerked his snout to the back of a house. *A little girl was being attacked, so they went back there to help her since the numbers had already been cut down.*

Vampires really were the most cold and heartless supernatural breed of them all. Killing a small child was the same as killing an old person. They didn't give a shit. *We need to shift back and take care of the dead.* It was the right thing to do.

I turned and trotted back toward Brent.

He was lying next to his wife, his head on her stomach. When he saw me, he raised up onto all four legs. *Is everything okay?*

Not sure if okay is the right way of putting it, but we all need to shift back. I paused for a minute because this was kind of awkward. *Do you mind shifting and grabbing our clothes from the Suburban? I'll stay with your mate.*

Yeah, I can do that. He ran into the house, leaving me alone with the injured woman.

I walked over to her and noticed her breathing was growing louder as if she was struggling. We needed to get her into a room and elevate her legs. If we could slow down the bleeding, her wolf should be able to begin healing. We couldn't lose her and the baby.

In what could only have been seconds, Brent rushed out

of the house and ran straight for the vehicle. He was no longer the cocky, arrogant bastard who came to breakfast. If it was under any other circumstances, I would relish it.

Guys, Brent's getting our clothes. Meet me over here at the house. We need to help his mate, tend to the injured, and bury our dead. I walked closer to the woman and rubbed my head against her.

Mason ran over to us with the rest of our crew following behind. It looked like Louis was the one who took the brunt of the injuries. Or, at the very least, he wasn't able to mask his discomfort like Mason could.

Thank God you two are okay. Kassie breathed hard as she reached me. *These vampires came here to die; a suicide mission. I don't know what the hell is going on.*

Brent hurried back over to us, holding three bags. "I hope these are all of them." He opened the door to his house, and we all entered. It was a nicer two-story house with an open floor plan and modern touches. It was even nicer than the house we had back in Columbia but still felt homey.

He turned down the hallway and went to the back. "Here." He opened the door to what must have been his bedroom and dropped our bags on the floor. "You can change in this room and in the connected bathroom there," he said as he pointed to a door, "and the hall bathroom.'" He pointed back down the hallway to a middle door on the other side. "Split up however you need. Please, I just need help saving my mate."

He ran out of the room and headed straight back outside.

Come on, Mason. I grabbed our bag with my mouth and trotted to the bathroom. *Let's change in here. You guys hurry. His mate is bleeding out.*

Okay, Louis and Ella, go down to that bathroom across the hall. Tommy grabbed the bag that must have had the guards' stuff in it.

Or, at least, I hoped it did.

I'll go change in the closet, and you two ladies can change here. He picked up their bag and went into the closet. *Let me get my stuff, and I'll slip it out.*

Needing to hurry, both Mason and I walked into the bathroom, and I shut the door with my snout. It wasn't long before we shifted back into our human forms and dressed. I wasn't going to lie; I enjoyed having to wear my yoga pants and a shirt.

"Are you three dressed?" I wasn't about to walk out to see things that I'd rather not.

"Give us another minute," Mona replied.

Hey. Mason's hands landed on my shoulders and turned me around.

Look, I'm sorry. I guessed he was going to use this time to tell me how I put myself needlessly in danger and everything else I'd done wrong.

No. He chuckled and pulled me into his arms. *I just love you and hate to see you get hurt. It kills me, but thank you for asking for help. You don't know what that meant to me.*

But you were already on your way. I hadn't been expecting this and was a little dumbfounded.

True, but you didn't know that. He leaned down and softly kissed my lips. *I love you.*

Even though I was responding to his kiss, a grin crossed my lips. *I love you too.*

"All right, it's clear." The door opened, revealing Mona. "Of course, I'd open the door to them sucking face."

"That's because you're too nice." Kassie opened the

bedroom door and motioned us all out. "If you just hollered at them like I do, they would've stopped sucking face before they walked out."

"Sucking face?" When she said it like that, it sounded disgusting.

"Yeah, it's an older person's term for kissing." Ella bounced into the room and winked at me. "It's the equivalent of bumpin' uglies."

"No, no it's not." Mona shook her head.

"None of these phrases sound appealing." Louis wrinkled his nose. "You Americans have some awful descriptions for things."

Tommy walked out with his forehead lined and brows furrowed. "This is a conversation I really don't think I should be hearing."

"Oh, are you like a hooker. You don't kiss, only do the deed?" Ella giggled as she took in Kassie's horrified expression.

"As fun as this is, I'm going to help Brent move his pregnant mate in here." I loved them, and I get we were losing our minds a little after that fight. However, duty called.

"She's right." Kassie pointed at me, clearly trying to get out of the current conversation.

Our group headed down the hall, and when we stepped outside, Brent had his wife's hand, and he was staring at her.

His eyes found mine. "What can we do?"

"First thing we need to do is get her into your bed and elevate her feet with pillows and covers." Kassie bent and was quietly listening to her heartbeat. "Thankfully, both heartbeats sound strong, so let's move her inside." She glanced at Tommy. "It'd probably be best if you carry her, just be careful, and don't jostle her."

I was kind of proud that I knew what she'd say. It was

the same first aid training they had taught me growing up. They did everything they could to make sure I could survive and thrive on my own.

"Okay." Tommy bent low and gently placed his arm under her head and her legs. He slowly stood up, barely jarring her at all.

"Wow, you got some steady hands." Ella nodded her head.

"You learn how to keep them steady when you have to help others recover from battles." Mona watched him walk inside. "Guards get hurt regularly, and it's not like we can go to the hospital to take care of most of our injuries."

It's sad, but I had never really thought about it.

"What can I do?" Brent stood, looking lost and helpless.

"Right now you should help find enough stuff to keep her legs elevated and pray that her wolf healing kicks in." I needed to help the others. "The rest of us need to bury the dead and help the injured."

"This is a nightmare." Brent dropped his head and glanced at me. "Thank you for coming to our aid. I wouldn't have blamed you for not doing it. Hell, I wouldn't have if I were you."

"Our decisions define us." I didn't want to be an asshole, but at the same time, he hadn't been on my side. He had fallen for Richard's false promises. "Remember that going forward." I turned my back on him and waved my group on. "Let's go. We're going to need a few shovels."

WE HAD to have been going for at least four hours. The moon shone brightly overhead, and I knew it was approaching midnight. My body was tired and sore.

"Go ahead, you two, go in and rest." Mona pointed at the alpha's door. "You both have been going at it harder than anyone."

"No, that's not right." I needed to be out here with them, helping the last handful of people.

"Honey, she's right." Mason took my hand and tugged me toward Brent's house. "The last two people are being tended to by Kassie and Tommy. Hell, Ella and Louis went back over an hour ago."

"It's fine, My Queen." The couple that had to be in their forties smiled at me. The woman's smile was sad, but there was so much respect filling her eyes. "I thought the last royal who cared for us was gone. I'm so thankful that I was wrong. You're just as wonderful as your father if not more so." Her eyes then landed on Mason. "And destiny knew what they were doing when they made you king."

Mason took a sharp intake of breath, and his eyes suddenly looked glassy. "Thank you, but I'm the lucky one." His attention focused on me. "She makes me a better man."

"Now, go on." The man motioned us away. "You two need your rest. All we have are a few scratches. We were the least injured out of the lot."

"Let me know if anyone needs anything." I hated to leave, but I was about to fall asleep standing.

"Come on." Mason began tugging me once more toward the house, but this time, I followed.

When we entered, I glanced down the hallway and found Ella, Louis, and Brent together in the bedroom, watching over his mate. I really needed to learn her name.

I turned and headed toward them with Mason right by my side. I couldn't imagine trying to do any of this without him.

Ella turned toward me when we entered the room and smiled. "I think they're going to be okay."

"Yeah, her heartbeat is getting stronger." Louis smiled even though there were dark circles underneath his eyes.

"You two need to get some sleep." The hotel was another thirty minutes away, so we were up for at least a little while longer. "We should be ready to go in about fifteen minutes." Even though it wasn't long, it sure felt like it was hours away right now.

"I have four bedrooms." Brent stood up and looked at me. "Please, stay here. You and the king can have the other bedroom on the main floor, and there are two more bedrooms upstairs. If your male guard doesn't mind sleeping on the couch, I can get a pillow and sheet for him.

That actually sounded like heaven. "Are you sure you don't mind?"

"It would be my honor." He glanced at his wife, his brown eyes seeming lighter.

I wasn't going to make him offer twice.

"That sounds wonderful." Mason's words were so fast it was as if he thought I might argue. "Is there anything you need from us before we retire?"

"Nope, not at all." Brent took in a deep breath. "I'm not afraid to leave her for a few minutes now, so that's a big step." He pointed at Ella and Louis. "You two go ahead and go to bed too. The bigger room is the door on the right. It has its own connected bathroom too."

"Sold." Ella grabbed Louis's hand and pulled him to the door. "I'll see you guys in the morning."

Despite Ella's persistence, Louis stopped in front of us. "Do you need anything from me?"

"If I don't get to go to bed right this instant ..." Ella ground out.

"No, we're good. Thank you for your help. Go get some rest." I couldn't even hide my smile at this point. "Everything else can wait until morning."

"As long as no more vampires show up," Mason growled.

"Okay, let us know if you need anything." Louis nodded at us and then chuckled when Ella began pulling on his arm again.

Soon, we were left alone with Brent. I wasn't quite sure what to expect.

"Go ahead and get some rest." He motioned in the direction of the room. "You both have gone above and beyond. This is the least I can do."

"That's damn right." Mason stepped closer to me.

"What he means is of course we'd come to protect our people." At least, you knew exactly where you stood with Mason.

"But I'm curious where Richard is." Mason tilted his head and narrowed his eyes. "He was your pick. Why are we here?"

"Actually, he was here when the vampire attacks started." Brent cleared his throat and glanced at his mate. "Let's go talk in the den. I don't want to disturb her."

"Okay." I turned, and Mason stayed right at my side.

I have a feeling this is going to be interesting. Mason linked to my mind.

We walked into the open foyer where there were a couch and a loveseat. I chose to sit in the loveseat so only Mason would be next to me.

"So, Richard was here." Brent took a deep breath and began pacing the floor. "He had received some kind of phone call that got him agitated. He got up to walk outside, but he was speaking so loud I could still hear everything he said."

Now we're getting somewhere. Even though I was exhausted, I had caught my second wind.

"From what I gathered, someone wanted him to do something, and he didn't want to. It escalated rather quickly. I remember him saying something like, 'Fine, I don't need you anymore. I've got the major alphas locked in to turn on her.'" He rubbed a hand down his face. "Then, he yelled, 'Yeah, right, what can you do?'"

"Any clue who he was talking to?" Mason scratched the back of his neck.

"No, not really. But it was someone trying to tell him what to do, and he didn't like it." Brent paused and glanced out the windows that faced the woods. "He came in laughing and remarked that no one could tell him what to do. Within thirty minutes, all those vampires showed up."

So not only do they have a witch helping in this but some kind of vampire too. The more we learned, the more nothing made sense.

CHAPTER FOURTEEN

THE SOUNDS of people talking woke me from my slumber. I reached for Mason, but all I found was cold blankets. He'd been up for a while.

My body was sore from the fighting and digging last night, but it wasn't anything I couldn't push through. I crawled out of bed and took a deep breath as last night replayed in my head. The vampires were somehow after us again. The last I'd heard, there was a bit of a vampire civil war as multiple people were clamoring to claim the crown. I'd hoped it would buy us time, but that obviously wasn't the case.

As I padded out of the room, I followed the sound of voices into the den. Brent and Mason sat on opposite ends of the couch while Louis sat in the love seat. The sacred scent of coffee filled the air.

"What's going on?" I took a deep breath, savoring the aroma.

"Uh-oh." Ella's voice sounded from the kitchen. "I better make another cup before Elena comes back here and kicks my ass."

"That's a valid point." I wandered over to Mason who opened his arms to me. I crawled into his lap, resting my head on his chest. My eyes connected with Brent's. "How's your mate?"

"Stronger." He let out a breath. "Her color is returning. Both she and the baby's heartbeats are strong again. Thankfully, we got her set up in time so her wolf could begin healing."

At least, that was some good news. "I'm glad. I didn't realize you were expecting."

"I try not to let anyone know. It's something that could be held over my head." He sighed. "Of course, the one person I had trusted outside the pack ran as soon as the first vampires appeared."

Yeah, I wasn't about to ease his conscience on that.

"Well, for being an alpha, you aren't all that good at reading people." Ella walked in, somehow balancing three cups of coffee. She headed straight over to me and nodded for me to take the middle one, which was being held up precariously by the other two coffee cups in each of her hands.

I sat straight up toward her and grabbed the cup of coffee. "Thank you." Those words were said with so much love. I moved to sit next to Mason so I didn't spill any coffee on him or me.

"It has nothing to do with reading people. He was just being opportunistic." Mason's jaw clenched.

I loved him somehow more for the fact that he didn't hold back exactly how he felt.

Brent took in a deep breath and nodded his head. "That hurts, but you're right. I deserved it." His eyes settled on me. "And I'm sorry. I'll be honest; I was thinking more about money than the well-being of my pack, obviously. But that changes now."

"I won't lie and say it's okay, but I'm glad that we're on the same side now." I couldn't be a leader, walking on eggshells, and Mason seemed to feel that same way. "Now we need to find time to go to Nashville and talk with the alpha there."

"No need to." Brent bit his bottom lip. "I'll handle it. He was only going against you because of me."

"At least, that solves one problem." It probably should upset me that he was the instigator of it all, but in that moment, I was relieved. We needed to quickly figure out who the witch and vampire leaders were before something else horrific happened.

"Did he give any clue as to who he was talking to?" Louis took his cup of coffee from Ella and sipped.

"Not really." Brent pursed his lips as he tapped his fingers on his leg. "He did mention that he had someone thinking they were more powerful than they really were, but that's about it."

The front door opened, and Tommy appeared in the den. His already dark olive skin somehow seemed even darker under his eyes. He covered his mouth as he yawned. "Nothing seemed out of place. I think you all should be good, but you'll probably want to ensure you have a few people standing guard until we know what's going on."

"Have you slept at all?" It just dawned on me that he was supposed to be sleeping on the very couch that Brent, Mason, and I were all sitting on.

"No, but someone needed to stay up and make sure there wasn't a second attack." He nodded at me and smiled. "It's fine."

Footsteps sounded from the stairs; soon, both Mona and

Kassie entered the den as well. They looked rough but more rested than Tommy.

"Everything looks okay?" Kassie hurried over to Tommy and took his hand. She stiffened, as if she just realized what she'd done, and dropped his hand before looking in my direction. "Just needed to make sure his hands weren't blistered from all the digging last night."

"Yeah, sure." Ella snorted. "Let's pretend we believe you."

Kassie's eyes narrowed at her.

"Nothing seemed out of place." Tommy filled what felt like awkward silence. "So, I think we're good."

"It must have been some kind of point made for Richard's benefit, ensuring he realized that he was not the one in control." That was the only thing that made sense. We needed assistance determining who the hell was helping him. "I know you all disagree, but I think we need to stop by home. See if Rose can help us."

"Elena ..." Kassie growled the words.

"No, she's right." Mason nodded his head and sighed. "We can't let our pride get in the way. She's already helped us several times before."

"Helped is a strong word to describe what she did." Kassie sighed, realizing she was about to lose this battle. "But obviously, you both have your minds set."

"I'll go make the flight plans." Mona's warm brown eyes landed on me. "I'm assuming we want to head out sooner rather than later?"

"Yeah. We need to go back and check on James's pack, make sure nothing weird has happened." I linked to Mason. *Have you heard from your dad?*

No, but he knows what we've been dealing with. He took a deep breath.

It wouldn't hurt to stop and check on our family. "Let's go back to the hotel and get packing."

As we entered our plane, the hair at the back of my neck stood on end. It felt as if we were waiting for the last thing to drop. I hated feeling like we didn't have at least some control over anything happening. The only good thing about this flight was that we wouldn't spend much time in the air.

"Yeah, we'll be there in about an hour and a half." Mason entered the plane right behind me as he talked to his father on the phone. "Okay. No need, they've already reserved us some vehicles to get there. We'll see you soon. Bye."

Everything okay? I could've probably eavesdropped on their call, using our bond, but I hated not giving him some privacy.

There are some odd things going on, but Dad wouldn't elaborate. He said he'd tell us when we got there. He took my hand and pulled me toward the couch in the middle.

The rest of our group got on board, and Ella plopped on the floor right in front of me. "When we come back, I want to stay at that hotel again. It was super nice, and they had our bags ready so we didn't even have to stop and go in."

"It's one of the better hotels, that's for sure." Louis took a seat a few feet away and grinned. He still appeared a little unsure of where he stood with us. Despite having already begun earning our trust back with his actions in protecting Ella and fighting the vampires.

"Hey, you." I stood and walked around Ella as I pointed

at Tommy. "Yes, this may be a quick flight, but you get the bed in the back. Try to take a nap."

"No, it's ..." A huge yawn cut him off.

"See, you can't even finish a sentence without trying to show me your tonsils." Ella scrunched her face. "Trust me, it's not a good look on you."

"And it is for some?" Mona chuckled.

"But it's your bed." Tommy shook his head. "That's ... not okay."

"You are family. I insist." There was no way I was going to let him fall asleep sitting up. "If you sit out here, you're going to fall asleep and get a crick in your neck. I need you in tip-top shape."

Ella jumped to her feet. "You know they're not going to give up."

"Fine." Something akin to gratitude passed across his face. "I could use a nap."

"And don't worry. When they started going at it on our last plane ride, I stopped it before anything could progress." She sat in Louis's lap and winked at him. "So you're good."

"They change the sheets between flights." Mason shook his head and frowned. "You know what. It doesn't matter. Please go get some rest."

Tommy nodded and headed through the back door, shutting it behind him.

"All right." The captain entered the plane and pointed at Mona and Kassie. "Please take a seat, we're about to take off."

Mona and Kassie followed the captain and took a few seats right up front. After a few minutes, we were in the air.

Hey, come here. Mason wrapped his arm around my shoulders and took my hand. *You've been quiet for a while now.*

Just mulling over everything that's going on. I leaned in to his shoulder and took a deep breath. He always smelled earthy and made me feel at home.

He turned his head so he could kiss my forehead. *If Tommy wasn't back there in that bed, I could be doing things to you that would help take your mind off all of that.*

That sounds very appetizing. Right now, I'd love to feel his body all over mine. I raised my head and brushed my lips against his.

A low growl was his response.

"Oh, hell no." Ella stiffened and wrinkled her nose. "Don't even go there."

"Sometimes you can keep your comments to yourself." Mason's voice was raspy with need.

"And see, that there is why I can't." Ella shook her head. "Louis and I behave better than you two."

Not wanting to hear her mouth the entire trip, I brushed his lips once more and cuddled into his side.

It was nice being able to relax for the short time in the air, but there was an uneasy feeling inside me.

Hey, what's wrong? Mason pulled me into his chest and kissed my forehead. *I figured you would've taken a nap.*

Something doesn't feel right. I didn't know how to put it.

Right then, the air attendant appeared and smiled at the six of us. "Good morning. We're getting ready to land. It'll be only a few minutes longer."

"Okay, thanks." I sat straight up and placed my hand into Mason's lap. "At least, we're almost there so we can figure out our next steps."

"I hope Mom has lunch made or something." Ella rubbed her belly. "This beef jerky isn't cutting it. I need some steak and fried potatoes."

"When are you ever full?" Louis leaned over and kissed her cheek.

"Boy, you better watch it." Ella arched an eyebrow. "Desperate times call for desperate measures, and besides, you've got some muscle on you."

"We don't want to hear about your foreplay," Kassie complained as she turned and looked over her shoulder. "Just shut it. Your mom always has things to eat, so you know you don't have to ever worry about going hungry."

The plane began to descend, and I couldn't wait until we landed. Ella got extra mouthy when she was hungry.

"Hey, I wasn't talking to you." Ella stuck her tongue out at Kassie.

"But the whole damn plane could hear you." Kassie shook her head.

"She's just being herself." Mona chuckled.

I was glad, for the most part, the whole ride had been in silence. We were all tired and needed time to settle in. Tommy was snoring, so I knew that he had slept the entire way. He deserved it.

The speaker dinged, and a voice came over the intercom. "Uh ... We have a slight problem."

My body tensed.

"The landing gear isn't working, which means we're going to have to do an emergency landing." The captain cleared his throat, clearly uncomfortable with the news that he was sharing with us. "Everyone needs to sit in a standard airplane seat and buckle up. It's going to be a ... rough landing."

Crap, the marble we had received on our way to Atlanta popped into my mind. It was in the carry-on bag beneath my feet. *We need to go grab Tommy.*

I'll get him. Mason pointed at the three chairs across

from Mona and Kassie. *Go ahead and get buckled. I'll be right there.*

I wanted to argue with him, but now wasn't the time. I got up and hurried to the seats, sitting near the window.

"Oh, hell no." Kassie stood from her seat and walked over to me. "Get up and move over."

"What? No." Right now wasn't the time for us to play musical chairs. "You need to be sitting down."

"You're right, and you aren't going to take the seat by the window." She pointed at the window that was about a foot away. "If anyone is going to get cut, it's going to be me. Now move."

My mouth opened to argue, but there was no point. If I didn't move, she'd stand in front of me, demanding for me to comply, and we'd both wind up getting hurt in the process. I stood and moved over to the spot I'd planned on Mason sitting in.

"Thank you." Kassie plopped down beside me and fastened her seat belt.

The back door opened, and a groggy Tommy and Mason appeared. Mason pointed to the open spot next to Louis. "Why don't you sit here? I'll go sit next to Mona."

"Yeah, okay." He slid past Louis and put a seat in between them so he was sitting closer to the window.

Even though Tommy still seemed tired, the dark circles under his eyes weren't as prominent.

The beep of the intercom came back on. "We will be descending in the next ten minutes. Please ensure your seatbelt is on securely, and assume the crash position. It's going to be a bumpy landing."

His last comment caused my anxiety to skyrocket. I tried taking deep, calming breaths as I leaned my head forward and placed my hands behind my neck. There had to be some kind of witch magic causing all of this. I knew it was, but that didn't make any sense. There was only one witch who knew about my personal fleet. And still, the possibility filled me with fear.

It's going to be okay. Mason reached across the small aisle and took my hand. *I'm sure the pilot knows exactly what to do.*

We only hired the best, so that wasn't what I was afraid of. *I know, but what if it's tied to the marble we found on the way to Atlanta?*

You think a witch is doing this. Mason sucked in a breath and nodded his head. *There is only one witch who would know this plane.*

Neither one of us uttered the name we were both considering.

The aircraft began lowering with the nose pointing downward. I glanced out the window, watching as the ground rushed to greet us. We were racing to our collision.

Silence filled the aircraft, which was unusual for our group. The aircraft hit the ground causing my neck to jerk and snap. I tightened my hold on it as we slid on the runway with sparks flying everywhere. Metal on the bottom of the jet scraped against the asphalt, sounding worse than nails on a chalkboard.

Right when I thought that the plane was going to catch on fire, we finally came to a stop.

The quiet was eerie until the cockpit door opened and the pilot emerged. His face was red, and sweat covered his brow. "Let's get off this damn plane before something else strange happens."

I couldn't say it better myself, but I had a feeling this wasn't just a fluke accident. It had to be intentional.

CHAPTER FIFTEEN

AS WE STEPPED out of the plane onto solid ground, the familiar smell of Columbia hit my nose, immediately releasing some of my anxiety and tension from our near-crash. The very fact that we were here had my heart feeling at peace. There were at least five emergency vehicle cars, and paramedics raced toward us to check on every one of us.

After they let us go, we headed toward the building.

"Holy shit." Ella raced down the steps and headed straight to me, wrapping her arms around me. "I wasn't sure if we were going to make it."

"I think we might have all felt that way," Kassie huffed, scanning the area as if she was looking for a threat to pop out.

Tommy and Mona were the last two who were released, and both of their faces were lined with worry. Despite what we'd just gone through, Tommy appeared to be a little better off than he had been before his power nap.

"Let's get moving." Mona nodded to the airport.

As we walked through the building, I noticed there was

hardly anyone standing around. It was still early, not even ten in the morning.

A Suburban sat out front with someone standing right beside it. When the younger man saw us, he immediately headed straight to Tommy and handed him the keys.

"Thank you." Tommy took them but didn't slow down as he hurried to the vehicle.

"You're tired. Maybe I should drive." Kassie reached for the keys, but Tommy dodged her.

"No, I'm fine. Thanks." He sped up, rushing to the driver's side door.

"That man ..." Kassie frowned and shook her head.

Mona scanned behind us and whispered loud enough for all of us to hear. "Hurry. Let's get out of here." There was an edge to her tone.

"I don't see anything odd." Kassie scanned the area, looking for whatever threat Mona had found.

"It's more of a feeling that we're being watched." Mona waved us forward, wanting us to move even faster.

As Kassie reached the vehicle, she opened the back passenger door for all of us to pile in.

"I'll go first this time." Louis jumped into the Suburban, closely followed by Ella.

"Go, hurry." Mona waved both Mason and me in. "Let's get moving."

Not needing any further encouragement, both Mason and I clambered into the middle row. Soon everyone else got situated, and we were on the road.

"So was that not peculiar to have that happen back there?" Louis asked from the back seat. "I can't be the only person thinking that whole thing was a little too convenient after everything."

"No, I agree with you." Mason turned his body so he

could glance at the backseat. "Magic or something like it had to be in play."

"We need to figure out who's in charge of all these attacks." My heart dropped as I thought that one of them could be the very person I'd trusted for so long. "Do you think we could stop by Rose's shop before heading to James's?"

"I know you and Mason are hell-bent on ..."

I cut her off. "No, I'm afraid you might be right about Rose. I'd like to go visit her and see if anything is strange."

"Wait." Kassie turned around, and her eyes caught Mona's. "Did she just say what I think she did?"

"That you were right?" A huge grin spread across Mona's face.

"Technically, she said you might be right." Ella arched an eyebrow.

"Listen here, blondie," Kassie growled, "she said I was right. Got it."

"Yes, she has it." Louis reached over and placed his hand across Ella's mouth.

"No, I don't." She muttered the words as she bit his fingers.

"Damn." He jerked his hand away and shook it. "You almost drew blood."

"You weren't complaining last night." Ella tilted her head.

"For the love of God." Mason rubbed a hand down his face. "Please, shut up."

"Oh, but it's okay for you and Elena to suck face and moan in front of us." Ella leaned back in the seat and crossed her arms.

"Anyway." This was a conversation that I did not want to have, especially with the two people who had raised me in the vehicle. "Do you mind if we do a drive-by and see what's going on first?"

"Hell, it can't hurt anything at this point." Tommy glanced at Kassie. "Just tell me how to get there."

For some reason, my heart grew heavy.

Within minutes, we were pulling into the small parking lot of Rose's shop. All the lights were off, which wasn't completely abnormal. She'd always had later shop hours.

"What do you want to do now?" Tommy pulled into a spot and glanced at the building.

"Let's see if it's open." I unbuckled my seatbelt and opened the door. "Sometimes, she'd have the lights off even though she was there. It was rare, but I always learned to check."

"Hold your horses." Mona croaked from the back. "You can't just go out there like you aren't being stalked."

It was rare for Mona to speak to me that way, so when she did, it made me pause. "But I want to go in."

"Then give us a second to get prepared." She lifted an eyebrow.

"I'm on it." Kassie's shoulders shook with laughter.

Damn, she can be scary. Mason's eyes widened as he glanced in Mona's direction. *Granted, she's right.*

She's scary because she isn't constantly lecturing me like someone here in the front seat. She uses it only when she needs it the most. You could never underestimate either one of these ladies. *They have the good cop, bad cop routine down pat.*

Kassie climbed out of the car while Mona squeezed past my open door. They both scanned the area and then waved me on.

Sometimes, I hated how I couldn't just walk out the

door anymore without someone checking everything, but it was one of the many sacrifices for the crown.

Stay beside me at all times. Mason got out of the car and hurried to the door.

"I'm going to stay here in case something happens." Tommy glanced at me through the rearview mirror. "If anything is out of the ordinary, rush back here immediately."

"Let's go." Ella leaned forward.

I turned and placed my hand on hers. "Look, it'll be quick, I promise. If we all get in there, we won't be able to get back into the vehicle and leave quickly."

"No way." She shook her head from side to side.

"Elena's right." Louis took her hand and pulled her into his arms. "We'll give them five minutes. If they aren't back out here, we'll go in."

"Fine, but a second over, and my happy ass is popping inside." Ella pointed at me. "Got it."

"Got it." I'd be willing to say almost anything to keep her ass in the vehicle.

I stepped out and made my way to the door. Though the lights were all off, it didn't faze me. However, when my eyes scanned inside, I felt something sitting hard on my stomach.

The place is cleared out. Mason reached for the door handle and yanked it open. *It's like nothing was ever here, to begin with.*

"The doors are not even locked." This was odd.

He held the door open, and Kassie breezed through before I could move. I followed behind her, still struggling with the fact that it seemed like the shop had been shut down a while ago.

"I don't understand." Maybe she wasn't working for the

other team. If she was, wouldn't she want to keep her shop up and running? Give the illusion that she was on my side.

"Unfortunately, we aren't going to find any of the answers here." Mason walked over to where all her herbs used to grow. "This doesn't make any sense."

"Has anything made sense the last few weeks?" Kassie snorted as she headed toward the back.

I followed after her, seeing as Rose had always run back here after she took my blood. I'd never been allowed past the threshold.

As I entered the backroom, I was surprised at how open it was. And once again, it was like she was never there. The idea had me thinking. "Do you think she glamoured the whole place?" Was none of the shop even real?

Kassie stopped in her tracks and turned toward me. "That would take a lot of power to do, and what would be the benefit?"

"I ... I don't know." I took a few steps closer to the door and felt a certain energy in the air. Something that seemed to linger. "Do you feel that?"

"It's magic residue." Kassie walked over to it and shook her head. "Holy shit. We shouldn't be able to detect that."

"Then how can we?" *Mason, you may want to come in here.*

"Because whatever spell was cast here used a ton of magic and power." She shook her head. "There was only one time I felt a spell that was this strong. It was at a ..." Kassie paused and closed her eyes.

"At a what?" I didn't like when she did stuff like this. It was as if she was hiding things.

"What's going on?" Mason entered the room and walked over to me. "Did you find anything?" He paused and narrowed his eyes. "What's that vibration in the air?"

"Kassie was just telling me it was residue from a powerful spell." I still wanted to know what she was going to say.

A phone rang, and Mason pulled his out of his pocket. "Hello?" He paused a moment. "Yeah, sorry. We had to make a quick stop before coming there. We'll be there soon, okay?" Another second passed, and he put the phone back in the pocket.

"Is everything okay?" I couldn't help but worry when his dad called.

"Yeah, it's fine." Mason took my hand and intertwined our fingers. "He was only checking on us, but I didn't tell him anything. I didn't want to worry him."

"Okay."

"We need to go." Kassie motioned for me to move out the door. "When you're close to magic this strong, it's never a good thing."

Not needing any additional encouragement, Mason and I headed to the door.

Mona stepped in front of us and checked the area. "Come on. Let's go."

As Mason and I headed to the Suburban, the uncomfortable feeling of being watched came over me once again. I glanced around as I climbed into the vehicle but couldn't see anything out of the ordinary.

I forced myself to sit back down and buckle up. Once we were all settled, Tommy took off in the direction of James's pack.

"You were close to going over five minutes." Ella leaned forward between Mason and my seats. "Did you find anything there?"

We quickly filled them in on what we had found, and within minutes, we were pulling onto the road that led to

James's pack neighborhood. As we passed by, I noticed there were several wolves patrolling the perimeter. *This can't be a good sign.*

No, something must be going on. Mason scanned the woods as well. It wasn't long before we were rolling into the neighborhood and the driveway of James's home.

I loved the feel of their house. It was a modern craftsman style neighborhood that backed up to woods.

The front door opened, and both James and Dehlia stepped out onto the small front porch as we climbed from the car.

Dehlia met us in the middle of the yard and threw her arms around Ella. "I hadn't expected to see you all so soon."

"Hey, Mom." Ella returned the hug.

Dehlia made her rounds, hugging everyone, and then Mason decided to get down to business.

"Has anything weird been going on?" His eyes surveyed his dad.

"Well ..." James glanced around the woods as if he was looking for an enemy. "Let's go inside and talk about it."

"That sounds like a plan." Mason waved us on.

The nine of us entered the house and headed straight to the den. With all of the nervous energy I had bottled up inside, I went and stood next to the couch.

Hey, are you okay? Mason stood next to me and took my hand in his. *You've been awfully quiet.*

I'm tired in every way. Sleep-wise, stress-wise, and feeling overwhelmed. If I couldn't admit my weaknesses to him, then I was screwed.

We'll get it figured out. His words sounded like a promise.

"So, what's going on?" As soon as we were all in the

room, Kassie stood by the window, staring out of it, keeping watch.

"Well, if no one is going to sit down, I sure as hell am." Ella walked over to the couch and sat down, patting the spot next to her for Louis.

Neither parent acknowledged Ella's antics. They usually smiled at her, but they both seemed as if they were in their own little world.

"We keep getting whiffs of vampires the last two weeks." James shook his head and glanced at the ground.

"Are they attacking?" Tommy went over and stood next to Kassie. "We saw several shifters on watch in the woods."

"No, they aren't attacking." James glanced at his wife and shook his head.

"It doesn't make any sense." Dehlia shook her head too. "We've had nonstop watches, and their scent is still being smelled throughout the woods."

"How many guards have been on duty?" Mona leaned against the wall as she ran a thumb down her chin.

"We have at least ten on guard at all times." James threw his hands in the air. "And that's the most we can have out there at one time, but they still manage to hide."

"Are they threatening you?" Maybe they were getting marbles like me. "Or leaving you messages?"

"No, that's what is so bizarre." James ran a hand along his neck. "It's as if they are watching us watch them. It's the creepiest feeling I've ever had."

"I hadn't thought of it like that, but you're right." Dehlia shivered as if she felt a cold chill run down her spine. "How can a vampire get past us though? There are so many shifters on point."

"And don't forget to mention how many different

vampires' scents we're catching too. It's not one person sliding past our pack. It's at least twenty of them."

"They must have a spell." Louis's eyes locked with mine. "There is a witch involved after all."

"Well, I guess it's a damn good thing we stopped by Rose's shop first and found her not there." Kassie closed her eyes and blew out a long breath. "Someone is using magic, and we have no fucking clue who it is or if there are multiple supernaturals working together. We need to find someone who can help us. Cloaking that many vampires and for that long is another huge-ass amount of power."

"You're thinking of another magical residue level spell?" That's the only way I knew how to describe it.

"Hell, yeah. Probably even more so than what was in that shop." Kassie shook her head.

"What are you guys talking about?" James's shoulders stiffened as he took in our words.

Mason quickly filled in his dad and then turned and looked at me. "Maybe we need to visit the coven. I mean, someone should be there. They normally don't move."

"That's true, but I have no clue where they live." That was something I could probably figure out though if needed. Supernaturals had to disclose their locations to other supernaturals in order to set boundaries. That was one reason I didn't have a problem with Rose using my blood when I thought it was for killing vampires.

"But we do." Ella grinned. "So we could go visit them now."

"Do you have to call or something first?" Louis pursed his lips. "In Europe, we have to give them notice."

"The covens here don't have cell phones." Mason frowned. "But they'll know we're there. We just have to show up."

"Then, there is no time like the present." I was worn out, but we needed to get something nailed down on our side. Hopefully, we could call it an early night.

"How trustworthy are they?" Tommy stood and cracked his neck.

"If I go with you, then you should be okay." James pointed at me, Mason, Tommy, and Kassie. "Maybe the five of us can go. She trusts me, so we should be able to get by without any problems."

"Why would a witch trust you?" Mona tilted her head and narrowed her eyes.

"Because we worked together a couple of years ago when the vampires went crazy. We had offered our assistance."

"But I want to go," Ella whined.

"No, baby girl. You and your mate need to stay here with me." Dehlia winked at her. "I was thinking we could bake some desserts."

Ella stopped pouting and pursed her lips as she tilted her head slightly from side to side. "Uh ... okay. I guess that works."

"I'll stay back too to help keep an eye on the family." Mona nodded at James. "It seems that the smaller the numbers are, the better."

"Yes, we don't want to come off like we're threatening them." James shook his head. "So the smaller the better, but I also know we need to protect my son and daughter."

The fact that he called me his daughter warmed a place in my heart that I'd never thought could heal. "Okay, that works. Let's go." It was important to meet with the coven that Rose was part of, but there was no telling what we may be walking into.

CHAPTER SIXTEEN

WE'D BEEN RIDING in the car for over ten minutes. Tommy was driving, and James sat in the front passenger seat, giving directions as needed.

Mason and I opted for the back seat—since it was usually occupied with Ella, Louis, and Mona—so Kassie could sit in the middle to keep tabs on the situation.

I reached in the back and grabbed our carry-on luggage, pulling out the last marble that had been received on the plane and slipping it into my jeans pocket.

Come over here. Mason scooted against the side of the backseat, sitting right behind Kassie. He turned his body so I could lie in his arms.

There was no telling when we'd have the next opportunity to cuddle in the back of a car. *Don't mind if I do.* I laid my head against his arm that was on top of the armrest built into the door so I could look at him. *Have you been to visit the witches before?*

That one time Dad was referring to, but other than that, no. He used his free hand to brush my cheek with his fingertips. *I wish we had more time to be like this.*

Me too. I closed my eyes, enjoying the warmth. *I'd like to say it'll get better, but hell, it seems to keep getting worse.* I hated that I had brought him in to this chaos. Still, without him here beside me, I wasn't sure if I'd have survived it on my own. Well, okay. I was being a little dramatic. I would have survived, but I was pretty sure I'd have come out of it more hardened and jaded.

None of that. He leaned down and brushed his lips against mine. *I don't know what you're thinking exactly, but it's full of remorse, and I don't like it.*

I just sometimes wonder if you'd have been happier if you'd had a mate without all this. I closed my eyes, enjoying his lips on mine.

Of course I wouldn't. He deepened our kiss as if he was making a point. *You're the perfect half to me. Destiny even determined it. I'm happier now than I've ever been.*

Even with vampires, wolves, and witches at every corner? It had been going nonstop since we completed our bond.

Hell yeah. He pulled back a little, his emerald eyes sparkling. *Do you know how bored I'd be?* He winked at me and lowered his lips again to mine. *At least, we don't have some couples' problems of not knowing what to do on a weekend. Granted, I don't think I could ever get bored with you next to me. There's plenty that we could do.* He growled as he deepened our kiss.

My body warmed as I responded to his touches and kisses in earnest.

"I never thought I'd live to see the day where I missed Ella," Kassie muttered. "She'd tell the two of them back there to cut it out."

"They still are newly mated." James's voice carried all the way to the backseat.

It washed over me like a cold shower. *Your dad is talking about us.*

So? Mason tried deepening the kiss again. *We're mated and married. We're legal in all the ways that matter.*

Still. I couldn't contain my giggle. *Let's not give your father a show.*

Next time I get you alone, there won't be any excuses. He pulled back, but his eyes deepened into a lust-filled hunter green.

You won't hear me complaining. I winked at him. Surely, he had to know I wanted him as badly as he wanted me. I lifted my head and quickly kissed his lips once more. *Maybe we can find some time soon.*

"All right, it's right up here." James's voice turned serious, and my body stiffened in response.

I sat straight up and glanced out the window. As expected, we were turning onto a road that was barely traveled. The trees became denser as we drove through the woods.

I'm surprised the road isn't well-traveled. Rose had come into town daily. This appeared as if it hadn't been driven on in months. It had to be glamoured.

"Are you sure it's smart going in with just the five of us?" Kassie sounded as if she was on edge. "I mean a coven of witches could take out a huge pack of wolves if determined, and we're going in with five of us."

"I promise you." James glanced over his shoulder. "The priestess here is a good woman."

"How can you be so sure?" Mason stiffened and took my hand. "I mean they were taking Elena's blood to get the vampires addicted to it."

"I know, but that doesn't make sense." James turned so he could make eye contact with his son. "You met her."

"True, but a lot can change in a short amount of time." Mason shook his head.

"Hey, wait." I lifted both of my hands in front of me. "We agreed to this when we left the house. Why are we discussing this when we're right at their door? They probably already know we're here."

I don't like the idea of something happening to you. Mason frowned.

He was starting to sound more like Kassie every day. *But we agreed to this, and we're here. This is a conversation that we should've had back at the house prior to leaving.* "It'll be fine. And Ella could find someone who knows where the coven is if we need backup." I pulled my cell phone from my pocket.

The Suburban was silent for a minute when suddenly, a tall woman appeared out of nowhere in front of the vehicle.

Tommy slammed on the brakes, causing the car to jerk.

Pain shot down my neck for a moment. I reached up and rubbed the back of my neck. That was twice in one day where we'd been jerked around.

The girl in front of us appeared to be younger with long ash blonde hair that fell in her face and down her arms. Her face was tilted downward, but her eyes lifted, staring Tommy dead-on. She moved slowly as her white, dirtied, formless dress hung down past her knees. "Who are you, and what do you want?" Her tone was deep and old. Fog began to build around her and us, making the air feel humid and thick.

James rolled the window down and took a deep breath. "I'm James. The alpha of the pack that lives here. I was hoping we could meet with Agnes."

"And why would she want to speak to you?" The girl

moved slowly over to the passenger side of the car, heading toward James.

"Well, we helped you with the vampires a short while ago and we're hoping you're willing to return the favor."

"Aah, so you're here to cash in a favor." The girl nodded her head. "We cannot harm anyone if that's why you're here."

"What? No." James shook his head.

"That's real funny coming from them," Kassie muttered in the backseat.

Within a flash, the witch was at her door, knocking on the glass. "What does that mean ... dog?"

I jumped out of my skin. *Holy shit. She moved fast.*

"She didn't mean it like that." Tommy used his usual smooth voice to calm the situation. "We're not here to harm anyone or ask for any favors. We just need some answers."

"All things come with a cost." The witch's smile spread wide. "Are you sure you want to pay the toll?"

"If it requires me cashing in on our favor, then that's fine." James glanced in the back at Mason and me. "Can you please allow us in to see her?"

"Fine, but you must leave your vehicle here and walk with me."

"This could be a trap," Kassie muttered.

"Then turn your vehicle around and leave." The girl narrowed her eyes on Kassie. "Our sacred grounds will not be spoiled by your vehicle."

"Let's go." We were here and talking with them. It'd be asinine to turn around now. I began climbing out of the car while Kassie mumbled under her breath.

Wait for me. Mason followed right behind me as we climbed out the side where the witch wasn't standing.

There's no telling what we might be walking into with such a warm welcome.

Tommy turned the car off and joined us. "I'll follow you two."

James's and Kassie's doors shut as we headed over to them.

As soon as I appeared, the witch glanced right at me. She took in a deep breath and shook her head. "You didn't tell me the queen was here."

"Oh, well, that's my daughter-in-law, and that's my son." James slowly pointed at us as though he was afraid she'd think his finger was a weapon.

"Had I known she was here, I wouldn't have allowed you entrance." Her breathing picked up as she took a step in my direction.

Mason moved to stand in front of me, which pissed me off.

She's got a problem with me being here, and you standing in front of me will only make it worse. I had to face this head-on, and he couldn't do it for me.

"The last time a royal was here, it resulted in the death of one of our own." Her words were tight and thick. "Why should we allow another one in this time?"

I had no clue what she was talking about, but her light gray eyes bored into mine. I had to say something. "It isn't a question of whether you should. It's one of whether you will. I'm not here to cause problems. Only to talk leader to leader with your high priestess."

The girl's face didn't change. It was a mask of indifference closely locked into place. She took a deep breath and leaned toward me.

It took everything in me not to lean away.

"Fine, but no one will be leaving with you." Her voice

was tight and strong. "Do not try to lure any of our members away by promises of modern technology."

"Promise." It was an easy vow to make seeing as I wanted to get the hell out of here as soon as possible.

"Fine; then follow me." She turned and immediately began walking through some trees instead of the main road.

Is this what happened last time? This was one of the nice advantages of the mate bond.

No, not at all. Mason took my hand, and Kassie walked right in front of us as Tommy took the back. *Granted, they all met us around here. We never went into their premises, just the outer edges of it.*

Tommy stepped closer to us with his voice low enough that only a shifter could hear. "Neither one of you is allowed out of our sight."

It surprised me that he was the one who said it. "Are you that worried?" Unlike Kassie, Tommy had never acted like this before. Unease coursed through me.

"I'm not quite sure yet." Tommy took a few steps closer and lowered his voice even more. "James trusts them, and that means something. But even white witches can be opportunistic as long as they harm no one and keep the balance of the elements."

"Don't worry." Mason tugged me closer to him so our shoulders were brushing with each step. "I won't let her out of my sight."

"The concern is for you too, my King." Tommy arched an eyebrow. "Our duty is to protect both of you. Not just her."

"But I'm more concerned with her," Mason growled the words.

"And you don't think she's more concerned about you?" Tommy shook his head and quietly chuckled. "You're mates, for God's sake, and you are now the rightful king just as much as she's the heir. So you're both our concern. Got it?"

When did he get so pushy? Mason complained into our bond.

Kassie must be rubbing off on him in more ways than one.

And now you're channeling Ella. Mason squeezed my hand as he shook his head.

Oh, come on. I stuck my tongue out at him. *Just because we've been busy and lost our sense of humor doesn't mean you can credit Ella.*

I guess that's valid. His smile dropped as the tree line began to open.

A large clearing appeared in front of us, and there were at least a hundred wooden houses within it. I'd never visited a coven before, so it all took me by surprise.

Even though the houses were made of wood, they appeared strong and well kept. They didn't exactly look like log cabins, but that was probably the closest resemblance. There was a larger home in the middle that I could only assume would be the priestess's home.

"Before we allow you past the tree line, all weapons must be left in this spot." The witch pointed to the ground right next to the tree line. "You don't need weapons, so they will be safe here."

"But what if a vampire comes by and grabs them?" Kassie's shoulders were tense and rigid.

"Vampires haven't been here in at least a hundred years." The girl laughed like it was the funniest thing she'd ever heard.

"That's not true." James's brow furrowed. "We helped you get rid of them a few years ago."

"They were trying to break through our wards." She

smiled. "They wouldn't have been able to, but we wanted them to remember to fear us. We may seem complacent, but we have nature on our side." She pointed to the spot again. "Now, put all your weapons down or you'll not be going through."

"But we got through to here with no problems." Kassie took a step away from the spot on the ground.

"Because I was walking in front, allowing you to come with me." The witch raised her head and crossed her arms. "You have one last chance before going through. I already didn't want to allow it when she appeared." The witch stared me down.

"I've never done anything to you all." There was so much hate directed at me. I'd never met them before.

"Oh, but your blood has done plenty." Her breathing increased as if she was aggravated with my mere existence.

"Let's do this." Mason tugged me behind him while Tommy and Kassie placed their guns and daggers on the ground.

Once they stood back up, the witch headed over to them and examined them from head to toe. "I don't feel cold energy from you any longer, so we're good to go." She turned around, scanning me, Mason, and James. "All right, the priestess is aware of your arrival. Let's go."

As we entered the clearing, it felt strange as no one was outside. As we passed by one of the houses, I glanced in the windows and met cold, gold eyes. *They're all in their houses so we don't see them.*

Yeah, they like to be kept from sight. Mason's jaw clenched as we approached the larger house, and the witch knocked on the door.

"Come in." A strong voice called out that sounded way younger than I'd expected.

The witch opened the door and waved us inside. "After you."

Knowing that Mason and I needed to be the first ones to enter, I pushed past Kassie and James before entering the house.

A low growl emanated from Kassie's throat, alerting me to the fact that she wasn't thrilled with me.

What was new at this point? The first room we entered wasn't a living room but rather a kitchen. There was a fireplace in the middle of the room with a black cauldron sitting within it. The counters were littered with drying herbs and spices. There wasn't a refrigerator anywhere in the room. To the right of all that was a large table that sat ten. A lady, who had to be in her late forties or early fifties, was sitting there waiting for us.

"I had a feeling you'd be showing up soon." Her eyes landed on me as she picked up what appeared to be a teacup and took a sip. "I've been dreaming of you and knew it was only a matter of time before you appeared." Her dark amber eyes held mine.

I wasn't quite sure what to say to that. "I'm sorry if I caught you at a bad time."

"No, dear." She placed her cup back on the table and pointed at the open chair beside her. "Please sit. All of you." Her eyes glanced back to Kassie, Tommy, and James.

"I'll leave." The witch who'd been with us the entire time headed to the door.

"No, Star." Agnes arched her dirty blonde eyebrow and pointed to the other open seat beside her. "You'll be part of this discussion as you'll be expected to know how to handle these types of things when I die." She leaned back in her seat, causing some of her long blonde hair to fall over her slender shoulders. Her eyes moved back to me. "How can I help you?"

Since she sounded blunt and to the point, I figured it'd only be wise for me to return the favor. "I need to see if you can help me figure out something." I reached into my pocket and pulled out the red and black marble with the double infinity symbol inside it. "I went to Rose, but I couldn't find her." I wasn't going to accuse one of her coven members yet. "So I was hoping you'd be willing to help."

"Rose?" There was a darkness in her words. "She's been *helping* you?"

There it was, all the confirmation I needed. Rose was someone I should've never trusted, but now, I had to figure out what her motives truly were.

CHAPTER SEVENTEEN

"WELL, I'm not quite sure it was actually helping," Kassie muttered as she crossed her arms across her chest.

"Oh, I'm quite sure she hasn't been either." Star shook her head and wrinkled her nose. "Of course, she'd be involved in this somehow."

I wasn't expecting this reaction. I expected to either run into Rose right away or at least have these people not thrilled with us being here. I moved to sit in the seat Agnes had pointed to.

Neither was I. Mason sat in the open seat beside me. *We don't want her to feel threatened.*

That was a good point. I sat in the hard wooden chair and locked eyes with Kassie. My eyes darted over to the chair.

She huffed and took the seat next to Mason while James and Tommy followed suit. Tommy allowed James to sit in between him and Kassie, probably ready to spring into action at a moment's notice.

"Enough." Agnes narrowed her eyes at Star, a warning

clear on her face. "So that's all you want? For us to look at it and see if we can glean anything from it?"

"Yes, please." I was hoping they could figure out something. I was almost sure it was mixed with a witch's black magic.

The witch took a breath and picked up the marble with her pointer finger and thumb. As soon as she picked it up, she dropped it once again. "Oh, goddess." Her eyes were widened, and her face crumbled.

"What is it?" Star jumped to her feet and glared at me. "Did you hurt her somehow?"

"What? No." I didn't know what had happened, but Agnes's features took on a look of pure agony.

"No, it's fine." Agnes took in a deep breath and closed her eyes. "It's just... I never realized this would happen."

"What do you mean?" Mason shifted in his seat so his whole side was plastered to mine. *If she makes any sudden moves, we run out of this house. Got it?*

"It's her, isn't it?" Star sat back down with her nose wrinkled and her lip raised above her teeth.

"What the hell is going on here?" Kassie stood, and her breathing was ragged.

"You aren't in danger." Agnes waved her off and turned her eyes to me. "But you are."

"That's why we're here." Tell me something I don't know already.

"May I touch your hand?" Agnes held a hand out, waiting for me to close the difference.

Be careful. Mason's words were thick with worry.

I slowly placed my hand in hers, not sure what to expect. Her fingers gently dug into my skin, and she closed her eyes as if she was trying to focus on my hand.

She better let your hand go soon or I'll be removing it for her. Mason's body tensed beside mine.

I wasn't quite sure what she was doing, but she was obviously searching for some sort of answer.

With her free hand, she reached for the marble once more. Right before she picked it up, her hands began to shake. Her mouth began speaking words that none of us could hear. Only witches were allowed to hear the words of a spell.

After a few seconds, she let go of my hand and opened her eyes. "This is not good."

"Agnes, please." James leaned across the table, his eyes seeking out hers. "What's going on?"

"It's unprecedented that we would turn on one of our own." Agnes's shoulders sagged, and her voice was full of heartbreak. "But in all truthfulness, she hasn't been part of this coven for over twenty-five years."

My heart stopped. "Are we talking about Rose?" If she was, this was worse than I had anticipated.

"Yes, unfortunately, we are." Agnes dropped the marble back on the table and shook her head.

"All she's ever been is heartbreak for you." Star shook her head and almost spat the next words. "Rose has gone too far. We should've killed her when we had the chance."

"I don't understand. She told me she was part of this coven." If she hadn't been for twenty-five years, that means she wasn't protecting her coven from vampires at all.

"She was." Agnes seemed to age at least ten years right in front of my eyes. "She was my best friend growing up, my sister really."

"Then why the hell is she causing problems?" Mason was almost rigid at this point. "And you're allowing it?"

"No, no I'm not." She blew out a breath. "She was the

witch we kicked out over twenty-five years ago, but in fairness, not all of this is her fault."

"Don't even try to give that excuse." Star slammed her hand on the table. "Let's be real, Mom. She has always had a choice, no matter if you want to put blinders on or not."

Well, okay then. At least, we knew Star was the priestess's daughter.

"How the hell couldn't it be her fault?" I hated how witches spoke in riddles. The only other race that was worse than them were fae, and thankfully, they avoided coming over to Earth as much as possible.

"Well, I had always been afraid that this day would come, yet here we are." Agnes squared her shoulders and met my gaze. "See, Rose isn't a full, one hundred percent witch."

"Say what now?" That didn't make any sense. "She did spells. The whole fucking shop was glamoured."

"I'm not saying she can't practice magic because she is mostly a witch." Agnes huffed, and her eyes darted to the marble. "But she's part vampire as well."

"What the hell?" Mason was poised like a snake. "How the fuck is that even possible?"

"Language, please." Agnes narrowed her eyes at both Mason and me. "Her mother had been bitten during Rose's birth. You see, a witch's natural affinity to the elements makes them not able to survive the change just as a wolf can't."

"Then, how the hell is she alive?" Kassie growled the words.

"Patience is a virtue." Agnes glared at her before turning her attention back to me. "Now where was I?" She tapped her finger against her lip. "So, her mother had been rushed here after one of our own found her in the woods in a horrible state. When my mother and father laid eyes on her, they both knew she was doomed. They figured the baby was too, but once Rose was born, well, she was fine."

"So you guys let her stay here." Even though my words may have sounded like a question, it was anything but.

"Yes, my parents took pity on the child. After all, it wasn't the baby's fault, and my mother made a decision she might not normally have done. She decided to raise her as one of her own."

"What influenced that decision?" I had to make sure I had a clear picture.

"Me. I had only been born a few months before. She was a new mother, who had battled multiple miscarriages." Agnes's lips spread into a sad smile. "I was her miracle baby, and Mom hoped that Rose was another gift from the goddess herself."

"But she was part vampire?" At least, now it made sense why she was so cold and callous. Vampires were self-serving and vicious creatures.

"At the time, we didn't realize it." She glanced at the ceiling as if she was somewhere else. "We grew up as sisters. Even though she didn't look anything like me, we were inseparable."

"When did you find out that she was part vampire?" Mason seemed to relax ever so slightly now that we were getting information and the atmosphere had changed to non-threatening.

"We were probably around five." She glanced over at her daughter and took her hand. "We were beginning to practice our magic, and she was already so much stronger than me." She shook her head and sighed. "I was afraid that she would actually become the priestess instead of me. I had been worried."

I had a feeling that things were about to take a turn for the worse during her tale, so I kept my mouth shut.

"The next day, we were running along the spring. I'd tripped and fell down, hurting my knee. It began to bleed. Rose ran over, full of concern until she smelled my blood."

"Let me guess; she wanted a taste." Kassie sat back in her seat.

"Well, yeah, that's the short way of putting it. When we got back home and I told my mom, fear shone in her eyes."

"Yet, you all agreed to let the backstabber stay." Star's words were full of vehemence.

Agnes pretended her daughter hadn't said a word. "You see, she was a part of our family at this point. To be honest, we never thought that it was possible for her to even be remotely vampire. Somehow during the birth, she was connected to her mother long enough to change a little, but not completely. Of course, that's when she and I both learned that we weren't sisters by blood."

"I'm assuming she didn't take it well?" I couldn't imagine growing up with a set of parents and finding out they weren't my own.

"No, she didn't. But she was afraid of that part hiding inside her. So we all pretended it wasn't there." Agnes sighed and frowned. "All went well for the next thirteen years, and to be honest, she flourished. She had control of her magic better than anyone here, and she found the love of her life, Wilmont, who was one of the coven members. He helped ground her and kept the vampire side at bay."

"A man?" Tommy arched an eyebrow.

"Yes, our coven is less traditional than some. We recognize that wizards should have the right to practice with us. Our group is made up of both wizard and witch."

"So I'm assuming something happened." The story couldn't have ended there.

"As with most villains, there is usually a trigger." Her eyes settled back on me. "You see, the young prince of the wolves came to visit us that year."

My heart sunk. "You mean my dad?"

"Yes, the oldest prince." She tilted her head as she stared at me. "Honestly, when looking at you, it's as if I was staring into his eyes. It's a little uncanny. As if he left a piece of his soul with you."

"He loved her very much." Kassie's voice was thick with emotion. "It wouldn't surprise me at all if he had."

"Yes, well, you see, as most young people do, they are prone to making horrible decisions." Agnes rested her hand on the table as if she was trying to steady herself. "Your father was very charming." A small smile spread across her face. "I'll even admit I was a little taken with him. He and Wilmont hit it off extremely well." She lifted her hands, spreading them outward. "Even though we are one with nature, we do enjoy the luxuries of life from time to time. And apparently, your father had come down with some kind of sports car."

"It was a brand new Ferrari." Tommy's face dropped to the table.

"Wait, how do you know that?" I couldn't believe he would hide something like that from us.

"I started as his guard right after the accident." He ran a finger along his mustache.

"Wait. That was a witch?" Kassie's mouth dropped open. "He'd mentioned it a few times when he drank too much, but I never really understood what happened."

"Can someone just tell me what happened?" I needed to know everything and now.

"Well, your father and Wilmont bonded, so the prince agreed to let him drive his car." Agnes rubbed her temples. "Mom should've said no, but a wolf prince never wanted to visit with our people before. It was an olive branch, and we were all encouraged that maybe we could be at peace with them."

Mason squeezed my hand.

We both knew what was coming next.

"So Rose and I decided to go watch." She picked up the cup of tea with shaky hands and took a sip.

I wanted to snap at her, get on with it already. Only, it was obvious she was struggling with the memory and her emotions.

Mason opened his mouth, and I cut my eyes at him, shaking my head no.

This can't be good. I felt it in my bones. *Give her a minute.*

"Long story short, not even a hundred yards away, Wilmont flipped the car over. It rolled over and over."

It sounded like the wreck I had with my parents. Could it have been purposefully planned that way?

"Rose and I screamed. We even used our magic to stop it from going into a lake." She took a deep breath as a tear ran down her face, leaving a trail of moisture behind. "But it wasn't okay. Your dad was injured, but Wilmont. He was dead before we got there."

"So that's when Rose turned?" The loss of her love being her trigger. I couldn't imagine how she felt. If I lost Mason, I'd go insane."

"That was the beginning of the end." Agnes wiped away the tear from under her eye. "She was devastated as was I. Wilmont was her lover, but he was like a brother to me. As each day passed, she became a fraction of who she was, allowing the dark vampiric urges to take over. It wasn't long before my mother passed away strangely. There were two small bite marks on her neck, but I foolishly refused to admit what was staring me right in the face. It took two years for me to finally even acknowledge what was going on."

Rose had killed her mother. The woman who raised her and loved her despite all odds. She was more of a monster than I realized.

"Members brought her odd behavior to my attention, so I couldn't keep the blinders on any longer. My coven was more important than one person even if she was my sister in every way that counted. I noticed Rose was sneaking out in the middle of the night. One night, I followed her and found her at the vampire prince's home. I wasn't sure what to do. I was standing there numb because, right there in the front yard, she was draining a human."

"Wait. The vampire prince." I'd been getting played by her in every which way that I went. "They weren't enemies?"

"Well, with vampires, they are never truly an ally." Agnes's face hardened. "They are only creatures who take advantage of one another to get ahead. That's when I couldn't deny what was right in front of me any longer."

"What did you do?" Mason was completely engrossed in the story.

"When she came back that night, I cast her out." Agnes's face fell, and her bottom lip quivered. "It was the final nail into her losing her humanity, I fear. You see, she blamed your dad for everything." Her eyes flashed up to stare into mine. "And to be honest, it was easier to blame your father. That's when we closed our borders and never let anyone in again. Not until you came today."

"I can promise you my dad didn't ever mean for that to happen." No wonder he was able to keep his feet on the ground instead of getting swept up in all the power like Darren. "If he was here beside me, he'd be telling you that himself and saying he's sorry."

"He had nightmares and blamed himself," Tommy spoke low, and something like pain reflected in it. "He'd wake up screaming his name. He never found peace about the accident. It took finding his mate," Tommy said as he glanced at me, "your mother, to at least keep the dreams from coming every night. His remorse was part of why I was so loyal to him. He was a good man who was haunted by that every day."

"You know, he'd tell me that each action comes with a consequence and that you did the best you could with the information you had at hand." I'd accidentally pushed a girl down at school during recess by using my shifter strength. It hadn't been on purpose, but everyone thought it had been intentional with the force I'd used. The principal had even called my father about it. I'd been waiting for a lecture. I cried as he walked me into his office, telling him I hadn't meant to. He didn't say a word as he sat in his chair and surprised me when he pulled me into his arms, giving me a hug. "Sometimes, accidents happen, and some may even haunt you. But as long as you do your best and try to do what's right, it helps define and mold you into a better, more sympathetic person. Know that some things may go awry and that others could be hurt unintentionally. He told me that no matter what, as long as your heart was good, hold on to the fact that you're part human and can make mistakes. Don't let those mishaps alter your strength, instead use them to move forward, doing the best you can. He told me to honor the memories of innocent lives that were stolen all too soon."

"I'm starting to realize how good of a man he was. He tried so many times to come back here, but we wouldn't bring down the barrier. And to be honest, I've always known it, but you being here seems like fate had a way of making things come full circle." Agnes took in a deep breath and leveled her shoulders. "You need to watch out for Rose. She wants you dead. You're now the closest representation of your father that she can hurt and destroy. She won't be merciful."

The one person I thought had been helping me for over the past three and a half years was the very one who was hunting me now. The problem was I didn't have anything I could leverage her with, so I wasn't sure how this could play out in our favor.

CHAPTER EIGHTEEN

THE CAR RIDE back to James's was quiet. I laid my head on Mason's chest in the backseat, just listening to the vibrations of the engine on our way home.

I'd hoped that we'd feel better after meeting with the witch. Though the situation was so much worse than I'd ever known. Not only was the witch I'd relied on the past three and a half years using me, but she wanted me dead. *It doesn't make sense. Why didn't she kill me before now?* None of it made sense.

That's a question I think we may not want to know the answer to. Mason's fingertips brushed along my upper arm. *But we need to get to the bottom of it.*

It feels as if everything possible has worked against my family. I hated playing the victim, but at the moment, I felt so stupid. *Kassie was right. I should've never trusted her.*

Honey, you were barely ready to take this on when we met. He kissed my forehead and sighed. *Imagine if you had tried at sixteen, without the support system you have now.*

He was right. Over three years ago, it'd been Mona, Kassie, and me. Now, I had so many more people by my side with the most important one being him. *Still, I was so stupid and naive.*

No, you weren't. He placed his pointer finger under my chin, lifting it so I had to look up into his eyes. *You were doing what you could to survive. And I'm damn glad that you did.* He lowered his lips to mine as he pushed his love for me through our bond.

I love you. The words were simple but didn't even describe what I felt for him. It was more than love. What I felt for him was so all-encompassing that sometimes, it felt hard to breathe and like I might combust. And to think I had tried to keep him at a distance for so long when we'd first met.

And I love you. He pulled back slightly to stare into my eyes. *Do not blame yourself for what's going on. This is not your fault.*

I turned and wrapped my arms around his waist, holding onto him tightly. I never would've thought I could be this happy, which was odd with all of the bad shit that was going on around us. However, a part of me had finally found peace. Now, I was afraid it might be taken from me. Rose had always been the hunter, and I, the gullible, naive prey.

We pulled onto the familiar road that led to James's subdivision. There appeared to be twice as many wolves running in the trees as there were before we left.

"Have you talked to Mom?" Mason's body tensed.

Something was wrong. I sat straight up and glanced out both windows.

"Just did." James glanced over his shoulder. "There are twice as many vampires here, and some aren't hidden. They're trying to break through the barrier."

Tommy hit the gas, and soon we were swerving into the

subdivision. He slammed on the brakes right in front of James's house.

My arms jerked out in front, catching me so my head didn't hit the seat in front of me.

"They need help now." James opened his door and shifted right away.

I jumped up and squeezed through the middle row, ready to get out and help too.

"Oh, hell no." Kassie reached over and grabbed my arm. "That's what they want."

"What are you talking about?" Did she expect to have a conversation right now when they needed our help? "We can't let them go out there and get hurt." I opened the door and climbed out.

"Babe, she's right." Mason stepped out behind me. He grabbed my hand and pulled me into his chest. "They are attempting to draw you out. She knows you want to be in the fight alongside our people."

"But I can't just stay here while everyone else is fighting." Did they really expect me to do nothing on the sidelines?

"Both of you are going to." Kassie pointed to the house. "So, in you go. Don't make me kick your asses."

I wanted to fight, but there wasn't a point. Tommy actually seemed to be on the same side as Kassie. I had to appease them and find a way out without them knowing.

Mason took my hand and pulled me toward the door. "We need to get you out of plain view."

You can't be serious right now. Out of everyone, I figured he'd be on my side.

Yes, I can. He opened the door for me and waited as I passed through. *How many near-death experiences have you had? And now we know that Rose wants to kill you. Do you want everyone else to get hurt while we try to protect you?*

Wow, he knew exactly where to hit. *You're right.* I entered the living room to find Dehlia, Ella, and Louis there.

Thank you. He tugged me toward the open love seat.

"I'm surprised you're all here." Ella liked being in the action as much as I usually did. "Everything okay?"

"Louis refused to let us go." She pouted and crossed her arms. "I tried leaving, but Mom ratted me out."

"The vampires increased their attacks after you left." Louis caught my eye. "It only makes sense that whoever was behind this would try to get either you, Ella, or Mason. Ella and Mason are the two best people to hold against you besides Kassie and Mona."

"He's right." Tommy nodded as he entered the room behind us. "We need to lock all the doors and stay inside."

"I'm going to go fight with my husband." Dehlia stood to leave, but Mona appeared in the room and shook her head.

"James made me promise that you'd stay here too." Mona sighed. "We had an inkling something like this may happen."

"What the hell? I'm the alpha's mate." Dehlia frowned and straightened her shoulders, ready to fight.

Right now, I understood exactly where she was coming from.

"He doesn't get to tell me what to do." Dehlia headed toward the door.

"Mom, I don't think you should go." Mason's voice startled me.

I hadn't expected him to get involved.

"And why the hell not?" Dehlia placed her hands on her hips.

"Because I understand where he's coming from." Mason's eyes turned to me, and he leaned his forehead against mine. "I've come close to losing her so many times; it messes with you. He'll be safer if you stay here."

"You think I'd distract him?" Dehlia's arms dropped, and her voice didn't sound nearly as annoyed. "It's not because he thinks I'm weak."

"Oh, God no." Ella snorted. "You're like one of the strongest people in the world. You were at death's door for how long, and still you refused to cower down."

"I hadn't thought of it like that." Dehlia headed back into the room.

At the same time, the front door blew open.

"Mason, get her out of here," Kassie yelled as a huge breeze filled the room.

Rose stepped inside the house as Mason yanked me to my feet, dragging me to the back door.

We've gotta get out the back door before she gets through here. Mason turned toward the kitchen, and I followed suit.

Do you think they're okay back there? I felt like a coward leaving them behind.

There are six shifters to the witch. They'll be fine. Mason opened the back door, waving me through. *She just doesn't need to get access to your blood.*

I hadn't thought of that. To me, she was still a witch. Would my blood make her stronger too? I hadn't even considered that possibility.

As I ran a few steps into their backyard, Richard appeared right in front of me, flanked by three large vampires.

Shit, this was what she had wanted. Though it was too late. We were here, and all four of them had their eyes set on me.

"Leave her alone." Mason's voice was a deep growl, and he stepped up beside me, ready to take them on.

"This doesn't concern you, commoner." Richard's deep voice was full of contempt. "I'm just here for Corey's little princess."

"I'm not going anywhere with you." If he thought I'd give up, he was about to learn that it wouldn't be that easy.

"Get her." Richard pointed to me. "But make sure she's alive; otherwise, your queen will get upset."

"Their queen?" That didn't make any sense. Who the hell were they talking about?

"See, you think you know everything, but in fact, you don't know shit." Richard's eyes narrowed, and a cruel smirk filled his face. "But don't worry. You're going to learn."

Without a warning, Mason launched for the first vampire, taking him by surprise. He punched him straight in the throat. The vampire stumbled several yards back and hissed.

"Get her. Don't worry about him." Richard looked at the other two vampires and pointed at me. "She's the one we need and want."

"Got it." The tallest vampire headed straight to me without a concern on his face.

He thought I'd be easy to take. Little did he realize I could kick his ass. I pretended to act nervous because, shit ... I was able to.

When he was within two feet of me, I squatted and threw my shoulder into his stomach, bulldozing him into the closest tree. A branch pushed through his chest, and his body immediately started to disintegrate.

"You stupid bitch." The other vampire, who had stood and watched the whole thing, blinked his eyes.

"I told you not to underestimate her." Richard shook his head and wrinkled his nose. "She wasn't born proper."

"If by un-proper you mean that I can kick ass, then yeah, you're right." I glanced to see that Mason and the other vampire were still going at it. They seemed to be equals as the fight was on an even keel.

Now I just had to kick this vampire's ass and take care of Richard. "Less talk and more action." I needed to strike hard and fast. It worried me that none of the others inside had come back here to help. There was no telling what was going on in the house.

The vampire blurred as he ran toward me, his eyes focused directly on my head.

He was either hoping to knock me out or punch the hell out of me. Either one wasn't good, but that also meant they didn't really want me dead like Richard said. What exactly did they want from me?

At the last second, I crouched and punched him in the stomach so hard that he lost his balance.

"Idiot." Richard rushed me with a crazed look. He was looking everywhere, and his eyes appeared dead.

These were the most dangerous types of attacks because you couldn't tell where they may target. They were only reacting and wanting to hurt in any way possible.

He reached out and grabbed my long, red hair in his hands, jerking back. My neck snapped, and pain ricocheted down my spine. Of course, he'd be the one to fight like a girl.

I spun around and clasped my hand on his wrist before driving his arm upward toward his head, dislocating his shoulder.

"Ow. Shit!" He cursed as he released his fingers from where they'd tangled in my hair. With his free hand, he clutched his shoulder, crumpling to the ground.

Checking on my mate, I looked in time to see Mason give the vampire another huge punch in the face. Blood was pouring out of his opponent's nose.

As I spun around to face the vampire I was still fighting, a hard fist punched me in the cheek, causing my jaw to pop.

Pain radiated throughout my head, but I couldn't let it faze me. I needed to get back in there and help the others.

The vampire reared back again, expecting me to be stunned. As he lurched forward, I dodged his fist and cut my hand up to hit him right in the chin. As soon as my hand pounded in to his bone, I heard a sickening crack.

His head jerked back, and his eyes filled with rage.

Rage meant adrenaline, which meant he didn't feel as much pain as I needed him too. Luckily, it also meant he wasn't thinking clearly. He reared back to hit me in the face when I spun around and kicked him in the balls.

A loud groan escaped him as he fell onto the ground.

"Why can't you just submit?" Richard screamed as he put his shoulder back into place and tapped into his wolf shifter speed to reach me. Fortunately, wolves couldn't run as fast as vampires, so he never became a blur.

He lowered his body, trying to use one of my moves. If he got me by the waist, I'd have a hard time getting away seeing as I was only half his weight.

At the last second, I spun away and dropped my elbow into the back of his neck and watched him fall to the ground.

You're having fun, aren't you? Mason had his arm around his vampire's neck as his eyes caught mine.

Kinda of, but we need to end this to get back in there to the others. I had a feeling there was a reason why they weren't coming out, and it wasn't going to be a good one.

Let's end this then.

I kicked Richard in the head, causing him to blackout.

Rose came trampling through the back door. "What the hell is taking so long? I can't keep them this way for much longer." She stopped when she saw the one vampire whose nuts still had to be hurting him stand and Richard passed out on the ground. Her eyes went to the tree where the disintegrating vampire was still turning to ash. "We don't have time for this shit."

"Oh, I'm sorry." She was acting as if we were making her late to a party or something. "Are we inconveniencing you?"

"Stop with the attitude." Rose rolled her eyes as the wind picked up, blowing her midnight black hair over her shoulders. She glanced over at Mason and sighed. "Why am I not surprised that both of you are still standing when you were outnumbered?" She straightened her shoulders and marched directly to me. "Let's go."

"Do you think I'd actually leave with you?" If she did, she must be on something stronger than my blood. "I know about your lover."

"Ah ... So you've visited good ol' Agnes." She shook her head while a creepy smile spread across her face. "I'm sure she was thrilled to tell you all about my story." She took a deep breath and frowned. "But all of that is history in a life that is no longer mine."

"Just leave us alone, and you can leave here without getting harmed." Mason yanked the vampire's neck to the left, breaking it. Then he dropped the vampire on the ground. "It'll be a win-win for all."

"Aw, it's sweet that you think you can win." She snapped her fingers, and ten new vampires appeared from the woods. "You see, over the last three years, I've realized how strong you've become and knew not to underestimate you, unlike those four idiots did."

Within seconds, half of the vampires blurred toward Mason while the other half came at me. They grabbed us by the arms and forced us to the ground onto our knees.

Except for the fifth vampire of Mason's pulled out a gun and placed the gun right against his temple.

Our bond flooded with fear before he cut it off.

"No, stop." I tried yanking free from the iron hands that held me securely in place. No matter how hard I struggled, I was at their mercy.

"Oh, now this is fun. You either agree to come with me willingly or I'll allow you the same honor as I had." She motioned to the vampires. "You can watch the love of your life be killed right in front of your eyes."

The vampire cocked the gun, ready to shoot.

"No, wait." I couldn't lose him. "I'll go. Just don't hurt him. Please ..."

"Elena, no." Mason's eyes widened. *You can't go with them.*

Do you really think I have a choice? I was going with them either way even if Rose was going to pretend otherwise.

"Damn magic." She huffed and shook her head. "I shouldn't have given you that option. Now, I'm bound to it. Fine, hold him down until I tell you otherwise."

The vampires dug their fingers into my skin and then turned. My feet stumbled until I forced my legs to walk with them.

I'm going to find you. Mason's words were strong like a vow.

You'll need the witches to help. I had a feeling that was the only way they'd be able to find me.

As I was forced into the woods, I could feel my mind fill with dread over what was to come.

CHAPTER NINETEEN

I WASN'T sure how long I'd been stuck down in this basement. It could have been minutes or days at this point.

When the vampires carried me off, one struck me hard in the head, causing me to stumble and they put a shit-smelling bag over my head. To think that the last minutes of my life would be like this was what I'd been afraid of for so long.

The thick chains that caged me were connected to the walls. They had locked both my wrists and even ankles into the cuffs. I could only move around three feet. A little straw had been strewn out on the ground for whenever I needed to do my personal business. There were no windows, so it was literally like time stood still. It was crazy; at times, I could have sworn I heard another heartbeat near me. I was so alone that I must have been hearing things.

Footsteps pounded on the stairs as a door creaked open. The light from the hall spilled in, causing me to wince for a moment before my eyes adjusted.

Rose entered the room with a superior grin on her face. "Well, well, well. . . How the mighty have fallen."

If she expected a reaction, I wasn't going to amuse her. I stayed put and glared at her.

"How are you doing?" She pulled out a dagger from her bag that she tossed on the ground. Her black hair was pulled back, and her amber eyes were light. She pursed her red lips and took a deep breath. "Mmm, royal wolf blood. The smell is heavenly. Unfortunately, your blood can't give me the same high as a vampire because of my witch part."

"Well, you're mostly witch, so that would make sense." That little tidbit of information filled me with relief, but at the same time, there was no need to keep me alive.

"However, it still makes me more powerful." She winked at me. "So don't worry. I won't kill you ... yet." She walked over as she examined me from my head to my toes. "This is going to be so much fun. Let's see, I could drink from your neck, but hurting you would be so much more satisfying."

"I haven't done anything to you." All these people hated me for things that weren't my own doing.

"But your blood has." She stepped up to me, her eyes locked onto my wrist.

I refused to back down. The more I acted like scared prey, the more she would enjoy herself. Luckily, I'd blocked Mason's bond to me when I got here. I didn't want him to worry.

She grabbed my wrist and pulled it toward her, sinking her dagger into my skin. She pulled the dagger from my arm and licked the blood off of it. "Oooh ... So good."

A whimper wanted to leave me, but I held it back, standing strong.

"You see, blood is one of the most important things in life. I'm kind of an expert on it." She flicked her finger up, forcing my body to slam into the wall.

Pain coursed down my spine, but I couldn't move. I was plastered there.

"After all, I'm an abomination. Hell, I'm not even supposed to exist." She licked off the other side of the dagger and cut her eyes to me. "You see, Agnes believes that I was turned during the birth process, but she's wrong."

I couldn't help it. I was intrigued. "You don't have to lie to me." If I didn't believe her, she might let more slip. That's what all the bad guys do at the end. They liked to spill all their dirty little secrets and frustrations.

"No, I thought the same thing until the day the great priestess handed over my real mother's diary. You see, she was never able to open it because it takes the blood of the witch or their descendants'. So of course, I was able to open it and read a lot of things that made everything clearer."

"So you didn't tell anyone what it said?" What type of person hid herself from those she loved?

"Don't act all superior ... bitch." She blurred as she appeared right in front of me and kneed me in the stomach.

I wanted to fall over, but I couldn't. I was still held securely to the wall.

"You came to me, trying to hide your own wolf." She stood in front of me and tilted her head as she examined me. "But her diary told me the answers to all of my questions. You see, my father was the one who had bit her, hoping to kill her and me. She wrote the last entry on her death bed in pain as she changed just in case I somehow made it."

"You know who your father is?" I opened the mate bond up to Mason. *Can you hear me?*

Yes, thank God. I've been going out of my mind. His voice sounded relieved at first but became more desperate as he continued. *Where are you? We have no clue. The scent vanished.*

I opened up to him more than I ever had before, needing him to hear what was going on. If I didn't make it, they would at least know.

"Of course, I do. But he didn't know, so I played that to my advantage. The night I killed him as he tried to protect *you* was one of the most oddly satisfying nights of my life. I let him know that some secrets can't be killed."

"The vampire prince." That's how she was the queen. Of course, *princess* wouldn't be enough for her. "But how didn't he know?"

"Oh, he knew, but he didn't think I could ever figure it out. He reminded me at every opportunity that I was worthless and a curse. He made sure everyone believed he was heirless, but obviously, he knew better. He looked at me with nothing more than contempt until I waltzed over to his house with blood; pure, genuine, queen wolf's blood." She laughed and lifted her head to the sky. "For once, the almighty vampire prince was knocking on my door and hunting me down. Between having control over him and manipulating Darren by not revealing your location, I was living the high life. It at least justified your existence."

Holy shit. This is bad. Mason's concerns flowed through to me.

"You were good for something until your mate forced you to set your wolf free." Rose spat at the floor as if she tasted something nasty. "And now you're here with his child growing inside you."

What? Mason's voice grew loud.

I'd thought I had been going crazy. Me being pregnant had never even entered my mind. Only now, here I was, bleeding and being tortured, knowing there was a baby growing deep inside me.

"But don't worry." She chuckled. "It won't be harmed,

for now. It makes your blood extra powerful, especially since it's a girl." She lifted the dagger and stuck it into my skin at the edge of my shoulder where it connected to my chest. "Isn't that almost like poetic justice? But unlike my father, I'll make sure you and she die when the time's right."

Pain pierced my shoulder, and tears rolled down my face. I tried moving, but all it did was make it hurt to breathe. I groaned as I attempted to just hold my breath.

"You see, that's only a small portion of the amount of pain that I felt when your father killed my lover." She snarled at me and dug the blade deeper into me before she broke out in laughter.

"He ... didn't ... kill ... him." Pain throbbed throughout my body, and I closed my eyes.

"It was his car. He should've known not to bring it." Her voice rose higher, filled with hysteria and hate.

Elena. Mason screamed through the bond. *Please tell me you're okay.*

Not able to handle his crippling fear with my pain, I shut down the bond again. However, when I did it this time, I felt empty and alone.

"But don't worry. Your daddy loved you so much there is a piece of him in you, and I'll get my revenge." She reared back, hitting me right upside the head, and then she yanked out the dagger. "You'll not only feel the same pain as me but more, by the time I'm done with you." She released me from her magical hold, and I crumpled to the ground.

"Elena?"

I could've sworn someone was saying my name, but I tried ignoring it. If I woke up, all I'd feel was more pain.

They needed to leave me alone so I could stay blanketed in darkness.

"Elena?" A hand touched the back of my neck.

Obviously, whoever it was, wasn't going to leave. I kept my eyes closed as the pain seeped back into my consciousness. I listened and almost cried with relief when I heard the second heartbeat inside me. I'd been so afraid I might have lost it. No matter what, I had to escape before I did.

"Holy shit! I can't believe this." Warm, strong hands grabbed my arms and gently turned me over, moving the hair out of my face.

My eyes cracked open once I recognized the accent. "King Adelmo?" Of course, he'd be involved.

"Yes, it's me." He huffed as his hands ran over my body, taking inventory. "No wonder they didn't want me down here."

"What do you mean?" My words were thick with pain and sleep.

"We've got to get you out of here."

I opened my eyes to find him glancing around the room, looking for some backdoor exit. I almost wanted to laugh, but that would hurt too much. Thankfully, my wolf side was kicking into gear, and I was healing. "Is this some kind of trick or mind game?"

"What? No." His gray eyes lightened, and his head shook from side to side. "I promise, I didn't know this was going to happen."

His smell stayed the same, and his heartbeat didn't increase. He was telling the truth for now.

I slowly raised myself to a sitting position. "Do you honestly expect me to trust you after finding out you helped kill my father?"

"My God." His mouth dropped open. "Louis told you."

"Yes, he did." What the hell was he expecting? "He told us when Atlanta's alpha, Brent, told me that he was going to start the process to dethrone me." I had a feeling he and Brent knew each other well.

"Look, I didn't know Darren planned to kill your dad." He lifted both hands in the air. "He asked if I would be interested in expanding my monarchy. He wanted to talk about collaborating so my kingdom had some influence in the U.S. Had I known what collaborating truly meant, I would've never asked for the impromptu meeting that weekend."

"Wait, that wasn't planned?" Hell, I'd been so young; I didn't really know our schedules or even care at the time.

"No, I called it last minute saying I was visiting from out of town." He ran a hand through his hair. "Of course, I knew he'd come. He always wanted an excuse to go to the Hamptons, but I'm sure you know that."

"I do." I scooted so my back was against the wall, helping prop me up. I didn't want to say too much and discourage him from coming clean.

"Anyway, I was shocked when your dad and the rest of you ran out the door." His eyes were glassy with tears. "And within twenty minutes, Darren was telling me that you all were dead and he appreciated my assistance on handling the situation."

That sounded like something my pompous ass of an uncle would say.

"And then he blackmailed me, claiming he'd tell the world what I'd done if I didn't give him access to whatever he needed." He pinched the bridge of his nose and huffed. "I've always lived with the guilt of that night."

"Well, your son appears to think it was more involved than that." Even though I hated to admit it, everything seemed to prove true. "So what are you doing here now? And why are you confessing to me? You made it pretty clear the way you felt about me."

"Richard called me in." He took a deep breath. "He said they needed help cleaning up a matter and brought up the pictures he had of me visiting with your father before he died. Hell, they even hired Europeans to run him off the road. They have it all locked up like I orchestrated the whole thing, and then my son willingly stayed with you. I'm sorry, but your family has manipulated and blackmailed me for the past thirteen years."

"No, my family didn't. They died." Did he think he'd get my sympathy for that? "My uncle and his family did. Did you ever think that Louis might not want to lead and that he might want to be here with his mate?"

"His mate?" King Adelmo's body seemed to sag. "It's that girl you're always with, isn't it?"

I hadn't meant for it to slip. It wasn't my news to share, but hell, we were having a heart to heart.

Two pairs of footsteps pounded on the stairs.

"Shit, I'm not supposed to be down here." He stood straight, and his eyes fixated on the door as it opened.

"What do we have here?" Richard walked in as the dim light reflected off his greasy black hair. "I thought you were staying upstairs."

"I heard a noise and came to investigate." He pointed at me. "She was crying in her sleep."

"Aw, are you hurting?" Richard cooed at me. He walked over to me and stuck his finger in the cut that was only beginning to heal on my shoulder.

It hurt so bad a whimper escaped me.

"Stop playing with her." My aunt entered the room looking like she always did; overdone makeup and heavy floral perfume. "We just need to figure out how to get something over that crazy-ass vampire witch. Right now, we're all little pawns in her game."

"Wow, you're lumping all of you in with me now?" I was surprised that she would be so willing to stoop to my level. *Mason, please tell me that you're there.* The tension in the air was so thick that there was no way this was going to end well.

I'm here, baby. In fact, we're close by. We finally found you. His tone had an edge. *What's going on?*

"Oh, hell no." She shook her head. "All I care about is Richard being king. He can't do that with you here and alive." She pulled out a gun and held it so it pointed at my chest. "So we can just take care of that now."

"Do you really think that's going to work?" I needed Mason to get here fast. This wasn't going well at all. The longer I stayed here, the more people either wanted to hurt or kill me. "She's a witch and a vampire."

"But we could at least have some kind of illusion of control." She cocked the gun. "Do you know how much I've had to sacrifice? I had to marry that buffoon, Darren, and get it into his head why we deserved this. Still, he had to fuck it up by not making sure you were dead thirteen years ago. This is the only way we can do that now."

Needing to talk to him one last time. *Just remember I love you.*

You better hold on. His voice was deep with fear and concern. *We're going to be there any second.*

It may be too late. I took a deep breath and closed my eyes. *Just know I'll always love you.*

Elena, what's going on? Elena!

She fired the gun, and the bullet sailed directly toward my heart when King Adelmo moved to fall onto his knees right in front of me. The bullet hit him in the back, going through his abdomen.

Adelmo. I thought I'd screamed the words out loud, but I didn't feel it in my throat.

He groaned as he clutched his side, and his eyes landed right on mine. "I'm so sorry."

Warm liquid spilled all over me, and the strong, rust smell of his blood filled my nose. There wasn't a way either one of us was going to make it out alive.

CHAPTER TWENTY

SOMETHING LOUD CRASHED upstairs as my hands searched for King Adelmo's wound with blood-covered hands.

"Mom, we've got to go upstairs." Richard grabbed at his mother and pointed to the door. "We can't let them get down here to her."

We're here. Mason's fear was almost palpable through our bond. *Where are you?*

I'm in the basement. No matter how hard I tried pushing on Adelmo's wound, my hands slipped off. *Adelmo is wounded badly. We need help fast.*

My aunt's cold, heartless eyes stayed on me. "Why do people keep protecting you?" As she lifted the gun at me once more, several loud footsteps pounded down the stairs. Right as she cocked the gun, Mason blew through the door and grabbed her wrist as the gun went off.

I closed my eyes, ready for the pain, but nothing happened.

"Dad?" Louis appeared at the door and ran toward the king while Tommy went straight for my cousin.

"What happened?" Louis squatted beside me and saw that I was covered in blood. "Did he hurt you?"

"What? No, your dad protected me." I lifted my hands, and they were covered in thick, dark red blood. "He saved my life. We need to lay him on his back. I think the gunshot went completely through him." I couldn't do anything with the blood on my hands, and my chains were holding me tightly in place, making it hard for me to turn him.

"I've got him." He gently clasped his father's shoulders and turned him onto his back.

A loud, piercing scream pulled my attention away. I looked up in just enough time to see Mason snapping the neck of my aunt before her body tumbled to the ground.

He flew past Tommy and Richard, who were still fighting, coming straight for me.

I stood on shaky legs as he pulled me into his arms, breathing me in.

"Are you hurt?" He pulled back, and his eyes widened in horror as he took in my bloody appearance.

"Most of this isn't mine." Yeah, that probably didn't sound very comforting. "Adelmo saved me."

"But you're injured." Mason didn't even care about the European king.

"Yeah, but it's healing." I used my right hand to point to the spot where Rose had cut me. "How long have I been here?"

"Two days." He spread the jagged edges of my shirt apart to look at the wound from the dagger. "Dammit, that bitch is going to burn."

I wanted to say let's just get out of here, but as long as she stayed alive, she'd always be hunting me. I was her obsession now.

"Where is everyone?" I'd expected to see more than those three.

"Agnes and the other witches are looking for Rose." He reached down to the cuffs and lifted them.

"Here." Tommy reared back and punched Richard hard in the face, causing him to fall to the ground unconscious. "I bet he has the keys." Tommy reached down and pulled a small set of keys from my cousin's pocket. "One of these should unlock them." He tossed the keys to Mason as he rushed over to Louis and his father.

"How is he doing?" I glanced over at them as I held my wrists out for Mason.

"He's losing a lot of blood." Tommy stood and ripped his black shirt off and tore it in half. "We need to tie this tight around his abdomen. Have to stop the bleeding."

"Okay." Louis lifted his dad upright as Tommy wrapped Adelmo's torso. Once he put his father back on the ground, Tommy leaned over and adjusted the material so he had it tied over the areas where the bullet wound was on both sides. "We need to make sure no one else gets down here."

Lighter footsteps pounded down the stairs as my wrists were finally freed. "Someone is coming."

"It's Ella." Louis glanced at the door as my best friend came through. Her eyes widened when she took in Adelmo, and then they landed on me. "Oh, thank God." She ran over to me but stopped short when she saw I was covered in blood. "How are you standing?"

"Most of it is his." I still couldn't get over how King Adelmo had saved me. "He saved my life."

"We need to get them out of here." Mason unlocked my ankles and stood beside me. "She needs to heal and rest." *We can't have you fighting with our baby inside you.*

His words made my heart flutter even more. I wanted to

argue. How could I ask anyone of them to fight for me when I wasn't willing to? Yet, this was about more than me. I'd already gone through so much stress, and I couldn't risk losing her. *Fine, but I don't like it.*

Of course you don't. He leaned down and pressed his lips against mine. *But you've got precious cargo on board.*

"We've got to get him out of here before someone else comes down and finds us." The first thing Rose is going to do when she's able is to check on me.

"She's right." Mason headed to the door. "I'll make sure it's clear while you five come upstairs." Soon, I heard his footsteps moving farther away.

"I'll go next." I opened the door and pointed at Ella. "Hold this for them, okay?"

"Yeah, sure." She took my place as I passed through.

The steps weren't anything like I expected they'd be. They were made of stone, and water dripped from the cracks in the foundation. When we reached the top of the stairs, there was a large, heavy, wooden door. "What the hell type of place is this?" My voice echoed along the walls. "It looks like something from way back in the olden times."

"It's an old, huge-ass mansion." A loud creak sounded as Mason pushed the door open.

I followed after him, and as I stepped onto the old wood floor, it groaned under my weight. *How old is this place?*

Over a hundred and fifty years old. Mason ran down the hall, and it was unnerving because we didn't cross paths with anyone.

The others appeared immediately behind us, and we took off toward the front door. As we walked through the living room, I found vampires all around, disintegrating where there had apparently been fights.

"Where the hell is everyone?" I almost expected

someone to jump out at every corner even though I couldn't hear or smell anything close by.

"They're all outside." Ella hurried and caught up to us. "Believe me. It's gory." She opened the door to a battle scene.

There were at least a hundred vampires to what had to be half the number of wolf shifters, and there was a group of ten witches who were facing off with Rose. The whole house was surrounded by woods.

How are we going to get him out of here? Everywhere I looked, there were people fighting.

"We're going to take to the woods in front and run as fast as we can till we can get to one of the cars we left behind." Tommy motioned for Louis.

"I'll follow your lead." Louis nodded at the guard.

Tommy took off straight to the woods with Louis following close behind while Mason, Ella, and I stayed behind to make sure no one could attack them.

We need to fight and help them. I felt bad leaving them all behind. My eyes landed on James and Kassie. They stood, side by side, taking on a group of four vampires. Yes, they were strong wolves, but they were still outnumbered.

No, we have to get you taken care of too. Mason took my hand as though he was afraid I'd run into the thick of the battle. *We have our baby to protect.*

But what kind of leaders are we if we run and hide. I hated to do this and felt like a coward.

You've been tortured for over two days. Mason began running faster, tugging me behind him. *And you're covered in blood. There is no way someone would call you weak.*

He had a point, and at the end of the day, if I fought, I could risk our baby. I took a deep breath and kept up. He was right.

Just as we were running through the thick of the trees,

something grabbed my arm and yanked me out of Mason's grip.

"Where do you think you're going?" Rose's hate-filled tone rang in my ears. She moved to stand directly in front of me and snarled. "I should've known they would go for you first and that Agnes was only a distraction." Her hold on me forced me to stand on my feet.

"Keep going!" I yelled, unable to turn and look at them. I couldn't turn my back on this bitch, and they needed to get Adelmo away from here.

"Why am I not surprised that Adelmo's injured?" Rose rolled her eyes as she closed the distance between us. "I have no clue why Darren and Richard were so determined to make him part of their plan. He was just a huge liability from the start, but at least, we may get a reprieve from him ... well, if he dies."

"Are you that heartless concerning everyone's death?" She was such a cold-hearted bitch.

"No, not one." Her eyes narrowed as pain filled them. "But you know that already. It's your father's fault all this happened."

"It was an accident." Agnes had made her way to us and stood a few feet away. "What would Wilmont think if he saw you now?"

"You bitch!" Rose yelled the words as she pushed her arms toward her sister and slammed her against the closest tree. "You don't deserve to speak his name."

Maybe we can sneak away. Mason appeared beside me and nodded toward the woods. *Agnes has her distracted.*

We can try, but she has it out for me too.

Agnes closed her eyes and lifted both hands in front of her. White power began funneling from her fingertips as it clashed with Rose's magic. As her power fought against the dark witch, it changed Rose's power to a black inky color.

How is that possible? Her power didn't have any color... at least, not until Agnes fought back.

Black witchcraft is meant to hide and sicken the mind. Mason took my hand again, tugging me to escape.

It's not going to work. Though instead of fighting him more, I turned to follow him again. As soon as I'd taken one step in that direction, something hit my back, making me fall to my knees.

A low, deep growl tore through Mason's chest. "Leave her alone."

"This isn't about you." Rose sneered, but then it turned into a creepy smile. "But when she's gone, I'll make sure you have someone to keep you company. I promise we could do things together that you never could with her."

Red-hot rage consumed me. "Do you really think that anyone would want to be with someone like you?"

"What the hell does that mean?" Rose pulled in a ragged breath as she took a step in my direction.

"It means you hate yourself so much that you take it out on everyone else." I was tired of being pushed around and manipulated. I'd thought as long as I didn't go for the crown, I'd be fine, but this bitch had been doing those very things to me the entire time I knew her. "You do realize you'll never be happy, not with how you let hate and anger control your life."

"Do you think that I care?" Rose lifted her head and stared me right in the eyes. "I'm Queen of the vampires. My father was so stupid, calling himself a prince when he could have been King." She huffed in disgust. "And soon, I'll be Queen over the wolves too."

"How do you figure that?" She was more psycho then even I realized.

"Well, when you're dead, your mate's right to the throne will be jeopardized. Or I could kill him." Rose scanned the fight scene all around us. "And then, Richard will be king. We'll be married and crowned together all at one time."

"Have you lost your damn mind?" Agnes closed the distance between us and stood on my other side as we faced down her sister together. "Do you really think you can rule as Queen of the vampires and wolves?"

"Of course, I can, and I will." Rose smirked as she tossed her black hair over her shoulder. "And then we'll take down all the witches and have you recognize us as your true leaders as well."

"That will never happen while I'm alive." Agnes's hands quivered with rage.

"Now, that can be arranged." She lifted her arm and pushed it out toward Agnes again.

Fortunately, Agnes spun, and the magic didn't hit her. Countering, she moved her arms and slid her hands outward, causing Rose's feet to be knocked out from underneath her.

We need to do something while Rose is distracted. I tried not to overthink things and ran straight at the witch.

Dammit, Elena. Mason began to shift, and soon he was running right beside me in wolf form. *Remember you can't shift.*

Shit, he was right. I was pregnant and couldn't risk miscarrying our baby girl.

"Ah, you wanna join the fun?" Rose's lips began to move, but there was no sound.

All of a sudden, excruciating pain filled my mind. I cried out as I tripped, falling to my knees.

Mason leaped at her, going for her throat, but she lifted her hand, and her power had him slamming to the ground instead.

A huge smirk filled her face until Agnes threw her hands up, causing her to stumble and drop the magical hold she had on me.

I quickly glanced at the fighters around us, thankful that our group still seemed to be holding their own. However, there was a wolf in trouble that must have been part of James's pack. Wait ... It was Alec.

Ella came bounding out of the woods in her wolf form, heading straight toward us.

While Rose was still down, I glanced at Ella. "Please, go help Alec." The last thing we needed was to lose a close friend.

When her eyes followed where my finger pointed, she ran off without any hesitation.

Agnes appeared right beside me again and still had her magic flowing out, keeping Rose down. "We need to kill her." Even though her words were strong, her eyes filled with tears.

She still loved the version of Rose she used to know as a child and a sister. Obviously, someone else needed to be the one to do it. "Got it."

The wind around us began to blow, and soon Rose was back on her feet. "Did you think it would be that easy to keep me down?"

Hey, Mason, Agnes and I are going to distract Rose. I need you to strike at the first opportunity. I had to figure out a way that allowed him to attack.

What I already understood was that she wanted my blood. I did the only thing I knew to do. I raised my wrist to my mouth and bit down so hard that blood began pouring down my hands.

"What are you doing?" Rose's entire demeanor changed.

"I figure if you want me dead, I might as well kill myself." I hoped she couldn't tell I was bluffing. I needed her to think I was crazy enough to do it though.

"What are you doing?" Agnes's voice shook a little, and her eyes landed on me.

"She wants me dead. It only seems fair. Then you all can live happily ever after." I reached up and pulled the ends of my dirty, stringy hair. "So, let me do the honors." I lifted my other wrist to my mouth and did the same thing. It was deep enough to where the blood appeared to be a heavy flow, but not enough to really cause death ... at least, not anytime soon.

Mason whimpered. *This better be an act.*

"No." Rose flipped her hand, jerking my wrist away from my mouth. "Only I get to kill you." She moved her hands to the side, and I fell hard on the ground. "You don't get to have a merciful death."

Mason, be ready. I slowly moved my hand underneath her magical barrier, bringing my wrist back up to my mouth.

"I said stop." She ran over to me, her eyes locked on mine. She pulled a dagger out from her dress and lifted it high in the air. She was aiming for my heart.

At the last second, Mason leaped, sinking his teeth into her neck. He pulled his head back, ripping out her throat, and her entire body hit the ground.

Rose gurgled as she fought not to succumb to death, but then she fell to her knees. All the vampires stopped fighting as if they had been under some kind of enchantment.

"No." Agnes screamed as tears streamed down her face. She stared at what was left of her sister on the ground. "Oh, goddess, no." She fell to her knees and reached out to touch the last little bit of dust from her disintegrating sister. "Rest in peace, sister."

The wolves stopped fighting, and they all turned toward me. That was our motto; if no one tried to harm, we wouldn't take senseless lives. The vampires obviously had been under some kind of influence or spell.

I glanced at Mason whose mouth was coated with blood. "We need to clear the area, and Richard is still in the basement. Let's get moving." I was beyond tired and just wanted to go home.

EPILOGUE

THE NEXT FORTY-EIGHT hours were a blur. The vampires were able to come together and settle on a new ruler. Now that no one in Nicholas's bloodline was alive, they chose a new family to take on the responsibility. Mason and I were impressed with their choice. The new leader, Liam, appeared to have more of a moral code, which was a welcome change.

When I'd asked about Richard that night as we were leaving the mansion, Mason informed me that he had died. I knew for a fact that Richard had only been knocked out when we left the basement though. Rose must have bonded him to her, which ensured that if she died, he went with her.

Fortunately, King Adelmo was on the mend. His wife and fae healer had been close by, staying at one of the hotels in town. Even though it was ultimately a fatal wound, Teague was able to heal him.

There you are. Mason walked into the bedroom of our brownstone home and made his way to me. *I was wondering where you might have gone.* He leaned down and brushed his lips against mine then rested his hand on my belly. *I can't wait until our baby is here.*

She's already being a handful. Even though I wasn't that far along in my pregnancy, I could feel faint little kicks. Shifter babies were stronger than human ones and we could feel the kicks earlier.

She, huh? His emerald eyes shone with love.

Yeah, I think it's going to be a baby girl. I hoped he wouldn't be disappointed if that was the case.

Even better. With his free hand, he cupped my face with his palm. *I hope she looks just like you.*

I love you. I stood on my tiptoes and kissed his lips. Sometimes, I couldn't believe how lucky I was.

"Ew." Ella shook her head as she entered the room. "I figured with Mom and Dad being only a few minutes away, you wouldn't be doing ..." she waved her hands in our direction, "that. Tommy said they're pulling into the garage."

Now that Dehlia was healthy and James had taken care of his pack, we made arrangements for them to visit here at our home in the city. "Come on, let's go."

We were planning to tell his parents we were expecting. Even though everyone here already knew, his parents didn't. That night, after all the fighting, was so busy; they hadn't noticed the extra heartbeat within me. However, now it was a lot stronger and undeniable. "Let's go."

Mason took my hand within his, and we walked into the living room as Tommy and Mona and Ella's parents headed up the stairs.

Louis walked over to Ella and wrapped his arm around her waist. All four of us were waiting for them to enter.

After everything had happened, not only did King Adelmo redeem himself, but so had Louis. He had been in a bad spot, to begin with, but everything between us had been restored.

When they entered the living room, Dehlia's smile grew huge. As she approached our group for a hug, she suddenly stopped in her tracks.

"Go on and hug them, honey." James laughed. "They aren't going to bite."

"No, do you hear that?" Dehlia's eyes widened as she focused on my stomach. "We're going to be grandparents."

At that very moment, I knew we were going to be okay. No matter what else life decided to throw our way.

The End

ABOUT THE AUTHOR

Jen L. Grey is a *USA Today* Bestselling Author who writes Paranormal Romance, Urban Fantasy, and Fantasy genres.

Jen lives in Tennessee with her husband, two daughters, and three miniature Australian Shepherd. Before she began writing, she was an avid reader and enjoyed being involved in the indie community. Her love for books eventually led her to writing. For more information, please visit her website and sign up for her newsletter.

Check out my future projects at my website. www.jenlgrey.com

ALSO BY JEN L. GREY

Wolf Moon Academy
Shadow Mate

Blood Legacy

Rising Fate

Bloodshed Academy Trilogy
Year One

Year Two

Year Three

The Half-Breed Prison Duology (Same World As Bloodshed Academy)
Hunted

Cursed

The Royal Heir Trilogy
Wolves' Queen

Wolf Unleashed

Wolf's Claim

The Artifact Reaper Series
Reaper: The Beginning

Reaper of Earth

Reaper of Wings

Reaper of Flames

Reaper of Water

Stones of Amaria (Shared World)

Kingdom of Storms

Kingdom of Shadows

Kingdom of Ruins

Kingdom of Fire

The Pearson Prophecy

Dawning Ascent

Enlightened Ascent

Reigning Ascent

Stand Alones

Death's Angel

Rising Alpha

Made in United States
North Haven, CT
02 November 2025